Joey

Joey

A loving portrait of Alfred Perlès together with some bizarre episodes relating to the other sex.

Henry Miller

VOLUME III, BOOK OF FRIENDS

1979
CAPRA PRESS
Santa Barbara

PRODUCTION CREDITS

Pasteup by Sarah Mollett.
Cover by Mary Schlesinger.
Compostion by Mackintosh & Young.
Camerawork by Santa Barbara Photoengraving.
Printed and bound by R.R. Donnelley & Sons.

Library of Congress Cataloging in Publication Data

Miller, Henry, 1881-
    Joey : a loving portrait of Alfred Perlès together with some bizarre episodes
relating to the opposite sex.

    (Book of friends ; v. 3)
    1. Miller, Henry, 1891-   —Friends and associates
—Addresses, essays, lectures.   2.   Miller, Henry,
1891-   —Relationship with women—Addresses, essays,
lectures.   3. Perlès, Alfred—Biography—Addresses,
essays, lectures.   4.   Authors, American—20th century—
Biography—Addresses, essays, lectures.   I.   Title.
II.   Series: Miller, Henry, 1891-   Book of friends ;
v. 3.
PS3525.I5454Z52   1979   818'.5'209 [B]   79-9304

    ISBN 0-88496-136-2
    ISBN 0-88496-137-0 pbk.
    ISBN 0-88496-138-9 lim. ed.

Capra Press
P.O. Box 2068, Santa Barbara, California 93120

TABLE OF CONTENTS

Joey

JOEY

PART I

Sometimes I called him Alf, sometimes Fred, and sometimes Joey. He usually called me Joey, seldom Henry. We met in 1928, I believe, on my first visit to Europe. I met him through my then wife June who had been to Paris the year before with her beloved friend Jean Kronski. Jean and Fred had met and Fred had fallen in love with her—"madly," as he always professed to do. As for my wife June he later told me he didn't think very much of her; she was to him a typical "Central European type," whatever that means.

As I came to know him better, during our years together in the Villa Seurat, I realized that he knew and was adored by quite a few unusual females. Oftimes he would stay at their hotel for a spell or they at his, which was usually a crummy hotel of which Paris boasts aplenty now and then.

The interesting thing about his relations with women is that they all *loved* him and adored him. He never married or even entertained the idea of marriage. He would talk as if he were *passionately* in love with each creature, but the way in which he declared his passion usually betrayed him.

It must be recognized at the outset that Fred or Alf or Joey was a bit of a rogue, perhaps even a scoundrel, *but* a lovable one. (I never met man or woman who hated him.)

He was born, so he always said, in Vienna, and indeed he seemed to retain a great affection for his native city. Oddly enough, my wife and I had visited Vienna the same year we met him in Paris. By this time (1927) Vienna had a woebegone look, the look of a city which had been through a great war. It was falling apart at the seams. My wife's uncle, who had been a colonel in the Hungarian Hussars, was now distributing reels of films by bicycle for a movie house, a job for which he received a mere pittance.

I have spoken elsewhere of the vermin of Vienna. Never in my life have I seen so many bedbugs climbing up and down the wall as in this famous city. And nowhere else in the world have I met with such wretched, abominable poverty. Some ten or fifteen years later I returned to Vienna with a Viennese friend from Big Sur. This time it looked somewhat better, but not much. It reminded me strongly of certain parts of my native Brooklyn, the neighborhoods I grew up in particularly.

Between visits I had spent some time in Germany. There I learned that the Viennese (and the Austrians in general) were not held in very high esteem by the Germans. They were always referred to as "treacherous."

I make this detour about Vienna to throw a little light on Joey's character, his origins, etc. From all he told me he came of a high class bourgeois family. He had received a good education and when the dread First World War broke out, he found himself a lieutenant in the army. Fortunately for him it was at this early stage of his career that a very important incident took place. I believe his company was defending a certain position from the enemy. The order had been given not to fire until one could see the whites of the enemies' eyes. Fred was in command at the time. As the enemy approached nearer and nearer Fred lost the courage to give the order to fire. A top sergeant, realizing what was happening, assumed command and thus saved the regiment from utter annihilation. Fred of course was court-martialed and promptly condemned to be shot. But his parents had influence with the higher ups and instead of being sent to meet a firing squad Fred was remanded to an insane asylum. He spent the war years as a lunatic. And then, upon the declaration of peace, the gates were opened and all the inmates rushed to freedom. It was then that Fred worked his way to Paris. He had had a French governess at home and consequently knew enough French to get by. (He also knew some English.)

From then on until I returned to Paris in 1930 to stay a few years, Fred led the usual precarious existence of anyone who possessed an artistic soul. It was also during these rather sombre days that he made the acquaintance of the various women who later dropped in on him from all parts of the world.

But, the time spent in the crazy house must, I am sure, have had its effect upon Joey's subsequent career. Though he never became a loony, he was definitely eccentric. *And lovable.* Always, no matter what his faults or defects, one had to add—*but lovable.* Was it at the bughouse that he read all the good books he later talked about? Certainly, by the time I caught up with him, he possessed a wonderful acquaintance with literature— German, French, and English. Of all the authors he admired or revered, Goethe took first place. He could quote him by the yard. Most of the celebrated French authors he also knew intimately. Both prose writers and poets. He began with Villon, then the 19th century "decadents" and symbolist poets—

Villiers de L'Isle Adam, Mallarmé, Baudelaire, Rimbaud, all the famous novelists and essayists. Samuel Putnam, who was something of a scholar and translator, always referred to Perlès as a scholar of the first water. Among German poets he was at home with Schiller, Heine, Hölderlin, etc.

Naturally, if one knew Joey, he made light of all this learning, or on occasion would even deny it to be true. As Joey, he was the clown, the "always merry and bright" companion who kept us all in stitches. He might be on the verge of tears, quoting a verse of Hölderlin's and the next moment guffawing like a jackass.

His countenance was almost always radiant, always wreathed in a grin or a benevolent smile. (Recently he sent me a photo of himself—same exuberant expression; not a day older in looks.) Only once did I see him angry. That was at Clichy where we shared a small apartment for a time. He was shaving and I, while watching him, was twitting him about his faults—mere pecadillos. Then I must have begun teasing him in earnest and I saw his face darken. Evidently I was laying it on too thick for suddenly he dropped his razor in the sink and swung at me. It was a good crack in the jaw I received and with it I tumbled into the (empty) bathtub giving myself a good crack in the skull. I immediately scrambled out of the tub and apologized to him. He then apologized to me—and soon ev-everything was "merry and bright." Nor was there ever a recurrence of this sort.

Yes, when I look back on these marvelous years together I see his face ever wreathed in a smile. One might call it a "Viennese" smile, as one often refers to a Japanese smile. As I mentioned earlier, Joey was a bit of a rogue, sometimes a downright scoundrel, or as we would say in America, a real son-of-a-bitch. (But, once again, a lovable one.) Elsewhere I have recounted (or did he?) how we robbed our friend Michael Fraenkel of petty sums. It was always a collaborative event. While I engaged Fraenkel in hearty discussion of this or that Joey would remove the wallet from the inside pocket of Fraenkel's coat (he always hung it over a chair when over-heated). To top it all, we would then take him to dinner — to his amazement — as he knew we were always broke.

When I became acquainted with Anaïs Nin, Joey naturally fell madly in love with her. He wrote her beautiful letters, dis-guising his passion: they were artful and highly literary, which was his forte. At first she inclined to look upon him favorably, never taking him seriously. But as time passed Fred became more and more infatuated. Despite all the women he had known, none compared with Anaïs. She was someone from another world, an ethereal world. He resolved to write a book about her — I believe it was in French. (He only began writing in English after going to England to live.) Unfortunately for Joey, Anaïs did not take kindly to the script he showed her. The reason? He had been too frank; he had mentioned names and circumstances which offended her sense of propriety. Or so she put it. Actually, what I believe disturbed her was his "truthful-ness." Anaïs, as everyone must know who has read her *Diaries*, was a very adept, adroit prevaricator. To use a more kindly word, she was a "fabulist," or "fabulator." I believe she was possibly more honest with me than with any other of her friends or acquaintances. But, well as I knew her, I cannot help but remark that she probably told me, too, some tall stories.

At any rate, Fred was now in disfavor. I use this peculiar expression because with Anaïs one was either in her favor or not. She was like a *duchesse* dispensing her favors or withholding them at will. Often one fell out of her favor over a trifle. To regain her good graces was like climbing Mt. Fuji.

Fred, who had put his heart into writing about her, was not to be daunted. He hit on the novel idea of, a la Solomon, dividing her into two different characters — one a dancer, the other a writer. He went to great trouble to accomplish this piece of literary surgery and once again brought the manuscript for Anaïs's approval. This time she was not only indignant but furious. Poor Fred was banished from court—irrevocably. (He never regained her friendship, I should add.) It was more a reflection on her than on him. I might add that later on Lawrence Durrell also fell out of favor, but he was either more artful or more persistent than Fred, for he won his way back to her favor not only once but several times.

What I think made Anaïs so hard on Fred was that she did not appreciate the clown in him. Unlike Wallace Fowlie, she did not make the association between clowns and angels.

Though at first blush Anaïs was always taken as angelic, I must say she was far from it. She was a very ambivalent creature, to put it mildly.

This time, to be sure, Fred was thoroughly crushed. He made no attempt to regain her favor. He simply abdicated. I think it was along about this time that a fan of mine, a Swede, used to come to visit me, always unannounced. He was probably the most frightful bore I ever met in my life. And, to make it worse, I didn't know how to get rid of him. He would stay on and on until we had drained the last drop from the last bottle.

If he happened to barge in on me while Joey was there, the latter would promptly get off his ass, reach for his beret and say, "See you tomorrow, Joey!" This happened a number of times before my Swedish friend caught on. Then one evening, after Fred had left hurriedly, he turned to me and said in all innocence,

"Meelah, why does he always leave when I arrive? Does he dislike me?"

"*Dislike you*," I repeated, "he despises you. He can't stand the sight of you."

"Why is that, Meelah? I have never spoken to him."

"Because, if I must tell you myself, you are a horrible *emmerdeur* (which is French for bore).

"And do you feel the same about me?"

I answered promptly—"I most certainly do! You are the worst bore I have ever known."

You would think that after this rejoinder he would either have socked me in the jaw or got up and left without another word. But no, instead he remained another half-hour trying to get me to explain to him *why* he was such an *emmerdeur*.

I have only known three or four Swedish men in my whole life—and they were all terrible, frightful bores. One of them was a renowned poet who translated some of the famous French symbolist poets into Swedish. We had exchanged a few letters and then one day he wrote he was coming to see me—where could we meet. I named a café on the corner of the Blvd. St. Michel and the street that leads to the Pantheon. It was four or five in the afternoon. I had looked forward to the meeting, knowing of his literary reputation. However, in less than ten minutes I had had a bellyful of him. All I could think of was what excuse to make and be able to duck. Finally I simply said that it just occurred to me that I had made a previous engagement for the same day, same hour. And with that I got up, shook hands and said good-bye. I remember turning the corner and walking towards the Pantheon, but soon turning down a side street for fear he might follow me. And that's that for the Swedes. . . .

Finally one day after I had been in Paris almost a year I got an attack of homesickness. I wanted to send a cablegram to my parents in Brooklyn asking for boat fare home. But I didn't have a cent to my name. I remember sitting on the *terrasse* of *le Dôme* and scratching a note to Fred which I put in his mailbox. It was asking him if he knew anyone who could lend me the money to get back home.

In a surprisingly short time he appeared at the café, sat down beside me and said, "Joey, you're not going home. I won't let you. Have another drink. Try a Pernod this time. It will pass. I've experienced this feeling many times. But you've got to stick it out."

Like that we sat, had a few drinks and soon were talking about other things, possibly about his beloved Goethe, his *Dichtung und Wahrheit.* Toward the end, he had a happy idea—he would get me a job on the American newspaper in Paris, *le Chicago Tribune*, as a proofreader like himself.

"Will I get paid?" I promptly asked, recalling my recent experience as an English teacher in the Lycée Dijon.

"Of course you will, Joey," he replied. "It won't be much but it will keep you alive." And on that we parted for the morrow.

It must have been shortly after this episode that I managed to rent a typewriter and began writing *Tropic of Cancer.*

From here on my whole lifestyle changed. I began to see the whole French world with new eyes. Bad as things were they were never as bad as in America. For one thing, I began reading

French in my spare time. I don't know how I ever managed, considering that my spoken French was literally atrocious.

Anyway, I had the good fortune to stumble on Blaise Cendrars's *Moravagine*. I remember vividly reading a bit of it each afternoon at the Café de la Liberté, near the Cimetière Montparnasse. To my surprise, Fred, who was acquainted with Cendrars's work, was not particularly enamored of him. Neither was Anaïs. To me he was a giant among contemporary French writers. I would ask every Frenchman I met if he knew Cendrars's work. As time went on I read virtually everything he had ever written. Often I felt I would go mad, reading one of his never-ending passages with the vocabulary of the editor of a lexicon. That was part of the charm of Cendrars—he borrowed from all professions, all trades.

But let us leave Cendrars for the moment. I will speak of him a little later, after I had finished writing *Tropic of Cancer*. Let me return now to another bore, this one an American from Topeka, Kansas. He was considered an expert in the advertising world, at least in America. He was pompous, vainglorious, a braggadocio and God knows what else. I had met him just once, briefly, at some reception. In the interim I had become acquainted with his wife who was a fascinating woman, a writer no less. She had already produced several books, one of them a biography of my favorite American writer, Sherwood Anderson. We got along famously each time we met. Then one day I asked her if she would not like to have dinner *chez nous*—I said I was a fair cook. She was delighted, then immediately added—"May I bring my husband along? I think you met him once or twice," and she repeated his name. I did indeed remember him and when I informed Fred of the dinner date I added "Let's show him a good time." From the moment Fred laid eyes on him he disliked him, couldn't stand him. Though he was an American, our guest, he had the appearance of Eric von Stroheim. He was arrogant, rude, and knew everything better than his fellow man.

I excused myself to watch over the *gigot d'agneau* I was preparing for our dinner. Fred soon joined me. Suddenly he whispered, holding up a bottle—"This is all the cognac we have." With that the both of us had the same idea—to piss in the decanter and serve it to this bastard as an apéritif. We knew that he was a lush and suspected he wouldn't know the difference. Of course, we were discreet—we didn't piss too much into the remaining cognac.

Well, we sat down to dinner and before tasting a bite I poured some cognac in our guest's glass and just a drop in the other glasses. We also had some delicious vintage wine to go with the food.

We watched his face as he emptied his glass—he just threw it down the hatch. He made a slight *moue* but made no remark about the foul taste. Soon we were all talking at once and devouring the *gigot*. His wife had begun to talk about André Breton, the pope of the surrealist movement. Suddenly her husband turned to me and asked very bluntly—"What is this surrealist movement I hear so much about? What *is* a surrealist, can you tell me?"

Blandly and innocently I answered with a smile: "A surrealist is a guy who pisses in your drink before he serves you."

With that his face dropped. He had got the drift of my reply instantaneously. (Besides, Fred was grinning like a Cheshire cat.) Without betraying his feelings he asked for his cane and his fedora, rose stiffly, a la von Stroheim, and bade us all good-night. Well, that was one bore I had really taken the measure of.

The joke was that his wife was not insulted; in fact, she seemed rather amused as if it served him right.

This little joke—a *bad* joke—was probably a hangover from my early days in Paris. Though the Second World War was impending and sensed by most everyone, still there was time to play. Indeed, it was just because of the disaster which lay ahead that people, particularly the artists, could launch all manner of crazy movements. Dadaism had flourished for a decade or more before Fred and I endeavored to start a movement which we labelled "The New Instinctivism." It was largely a movement *agin* everything. I think I mentioned elsewhere how Joey had endeavored to put over his (or our) crazy ideas in Samuel Putnam's serious literary review, *The New Review*. This was the kind of bad joke typical of the times.

It was probably my third year in Paris. Almost from the start I had begun writing the *Tropic of Cancer*. At last it was finished. But before thinking about a publisher, I knew it had to be edited, trimmed down especially. I looked about me in vain for editorial guidance. Anaïs Nin was out of the question. It was not her type of book. One day, perhaps at Fred's own suggestion, I asked him if he would help me. He immediately agreed. We were still proofreaders for the Paris edition of the *Chicago Tribune*, which meant we worked from 8:00 or 9:00 P.M. till 2:00 or 3:00 A.M. And then an hour's swift walk home. During the "break," around midnight, all of us except the printers used to repair for a drink to a café called "Les Trois Cadets" on the rue Lafayette.

I don't recall anymore for what reason, but we decided that

we would edit the *Cancer* book in the afternoons at this same café. It was a lucky choice for after a few sessions we noticed that we were very attentively watched by a dwarf who frequented the café everyday at the same time. One day we broke into conversation with him. We soon learned he was bilingual and not only that but a bit gaga to boot. Just made to order for us. Especially the rapport between him and Fred. (Now we had two Joeys.) If our little friend was a trifle gaga he was also something of a scholar. He knew all about the surrealist writers and painters and even professed to know André Breton himself. Fred and I were naturally more attuned to the Dadaists than the surrealists. Talking to one another about my script at the café we resembled a trio of comedians working out a new script. We seemed to do nothing but laugh and joke—*and drink.* Nevertheless the day arrived when we actually finished the job. We had mixed feelings—one of joy about finishing the work and one of sorrow that the three of us had to part. The dwarf took it best of all. He said we would probably all meet one evening at the *Cirque Medrano* where he was going to put on an act with some monkeys from the jungles of Brazil.

Three or four years after the publication of *Cancer* Fred had two of his books published in French. One was *Sentiments Limitrophes* and the other *Le Quatuor en Ré Majeur.* With neither of these was I able to lend him a helping hand. Poor though my French was I read these two books and appreciated them thoroughly. He said he had written before (in German) but I believe with these two books he broke the ice. Of course they did not become best sellers but he did receive excellent reviews from the French critics and personal tributes from some of France's top writers.

Somewhere in between these two events I wrote a pamphlet

intended to help him out of his economic misery; it was entitled *What Are You Going to Do About Alf?* We sent leaflets
and letters about this *plaquette* to a number of prominent
French and British authors. The idea was to raise contributions
so that Alf might go live in Ibiza or some other sunny and more
hospitable clime. To our amazement we received contributions
from André Gide and Aldous Huxley, among others. Here I
must confess playing a dirty trick upon my beloved *copain*. As
the return mail was addressed care of Henry Miller it was I who
opened the mail. Being rather hard up myself, I took the liberty
of filching the contributions at times, vowing that I would
make up for them when I got on my feet. (Which I never did all
the time I lived in France. I remember distinctly arriving in
N.Y. from Greece, with my steamer trunk as security and not a
cent in any pockets. Indeed, the first thing I did on entering my
hotel room was to call one of my old friends and ask for a quick
loan of a few bucks.)

I must say Fred took my pilfering in good spirit. He probably
would have done the same had the situation been reversed. He
was also very grateful for the meals and drinks he shared when
I at last became established at the Villa Seurat.

Somewhere about this time, or was it after the publication of
Cancer, which took a year or two, Lawrence Durrell wrote me
from Greece. He was enamored of the *Tropic of Cancer* and
threatened to visit me soon.

And he did. Fred was there when he arrived and the three of
us hit it off immediately. Though in his later writings Durrell
became a hermetic writer, in character and behavior at *this*
point in his career, he was a jolly, lusty Dada-surrealist son-
of-a-bitch like Joey and myself. To go with him to the cinema
was bound to be a treat. For, when Durrell started laughing the

whole theatre broke into a laugh. Once or twice we were requested to leave the movie. (How strangely similar was the deliberate surrealist act of going to the cinema and suddenly opening a basket noisily to produce some sandwiches and uncork a bottle of *vin rouge* and begin to talk loudly.) At this sort of shenanigans Joey was made to order. For example, if the three of us went for a walk and happened to be in the vicinity of a *commissariat* or police station, Joey would suddenly dart ahead of us, mount the steps leading to the station (the door of which was usually wide open) and shout at the top of his lungs: *"Je vous emmerde tous! Salauds! Imbéciles!"* Then he would quickly run down the steps beckoning us to follow, which we would do leisurely, only to find him standing at the corner quietly smoking his *Gaulois Bleu.* At that period, and I assume for many many years, the French police were hated and despised by the ordinary citizens, especially the youth. They were recruited largely from the mountainous Auvergne region and were naturally of peasant stock with insensitive hides. To do what Joey did was therefore tantamount to running the gauntlet. He would do these things to show off, to prove to us that though he was not a *costaud* he was fearless just the same. Also because he despised the Paris police. In addition to being a clown, a buffoon, a wit and a *bon copain,* there is no doubt that Joey was also a zany. During the period that Durrell and his wife stayed in Paris—a year or two—most every night was a gala night. Oddly, or perhaps not so oddly, Anaïs never participated in any of these riotous *soirées.* For one thing, she was not a drinker. (She could more easily have been tempted to try opium.) Also, as I may have hinted before, she loathed vulgarity and boisterousness. And these gala evenings of ours were anything but refined. Incidentally, it was noticeable that Durrell's wife was never present either. If she had, I am afraid it may have been disastrous. They had hot tempers and were not above using their fists on one another.

There was one evening in particular which I shall never forget. I believe there were just the three of us. I had made the dinner and the others had furnished the wines and cognac. (On these occasions we drank only the best wines.) It was the period when Hitler was causing a commotion everywhere. Sometimes Joey and I ventured out to hear him in some public place—over the radio, to be sure. We listened for enjoyment, I must confess, because of his atrocious German. Going home Joey would imitate his speech—he could do it marvelously.

And so, on this particular evening at the Villa Seurat, Durrell egged Joey on, plying him with liquor and laughing his head off at every fool remark Joey made. Joey had risen from his seat and was prancing about the room. Suddenly he knocked a bottle over, broke a few glasses (in his hilarity) and with this became even more grotesque than ever. For some reason he was in bare feet. When the accident occurred he was at first unaware that the floor was covered with broken glass. He only noticed it when he observed the blood streaming from the cuts in his feet. This seemed to make him more elated, more gaga. Now he began singing in German as he continued to prance about the table. Each time around he had another good sip of wine, cognac or whatever. Now he imitated Hitler frenziedly to our great amusement. (By the way, civilized creatures that we were, no one thought to stop the bleeding or beg him to stop his crazy antics. Durrell and I were by this time hysterical with laughter. We never dreamed of begging him to look after his cuts and bruises.) "More, more!" we kept shouting. And more we got! Now he began reciting German poetry, good and bad.

We all joined in singing *"Die Lorelei"* and other well-known German songs.

Finally Joey collapsed on the couch, his feet looking as if he had been crucified.

Durrell left to return to his lair and I went to bed in the next room. The place looked frightful, what with the uneaten food, the broken glass, the bottles on the floor, and the blood stains just everywhere.

I awoke about six in the morning on hearing Joey pass through my bedroom to go to the bathroom. He acted as if he could not understand what had happened.

He muttered to himself, something about vomiting and falling off the couch into his own vomit. Next morning when the *femme de menage* came to clean up, she was thoroughly horrified. She told me she had always taken me to be a gentleman *but* — such a pig sty, no, she had never seen anything like it in her life. I assuaged her feelings by giving her a good tip and she quieted down. (With the French, no matter what station in life, a few francs always work wonders.)

Today, after the frightful carnage of the Second World War it seems impossible that that monster Hitler could have unknowingly provided us with such a glorious evening. It's hard to believe that once upon a time he was just a nasty joke. But such is life, alas.

PART II

It was about the time that his *Sentiments Limitrophes* was published and reviewed in the literary chronicles that he received a wonderful letter from Roger Martin du Gard, a writer whom he revered. It was the sort of recognition he longed for and deserved and it put him in a state of ecstasy.

He was no longer living in the Hotel Central but was now a house guest at the apartment of a mutual friend named Eugene Delacourt. Eugene was a poet of sorts who expressed great admiration for both my work and Fred's. He was a good fellow in every respect except for one little fault—he had no sense of humor. At best I have seen a flickering smile hover about his lips. But he was warm-hearted, sympathetic and extremely generous.

In addition to these virtues he had a raven-haired mistress, Ariadne, who was something of a sculptress. The four of us often ate dinner in some modest restaurant and from there to the cinema or to a familiar café. Eugene incidentally picked up the tab—for everything.

One evening he announces in his usual grave manner that his grandfather had just died and that he would be leaving in the morning to attend the funeral ceremonies. He was going to the Isle d'Oléron in the south of France and might not be back for three or four days.

Hearing this sombre news Fred promptly said he would come stay with me until Eugene returned.

"Why would you do that?" queried Eugene.

"To avoid complications," Fred promptly replied.

"Nonsense!" exclaimed Eugene. "I want you to remain and look after Ariadne."

"Are you sure you can trust me?" says Fred.

"What are you talking about—of course I can trust you. *Nous sommes des amies, quoi.*"

Nothing more was said. The next morning early Eugene left for the south. By noon Fred was already in bed with his dark-haired ward. On the third day, in the evening, Fred comes to my place in the Villa Seurat with his charge, Ariadne. The two of them were all smiles—and why not since they had been fucking their heads off ever since Eugene left for the country.

We chatted for a while and then Ariadne seated herself on the couch in my studio, with her back to the wall. We were drinking a cool white wine and getting very *amoureux*, the three of us. Suddenly I leaned over her and planted a few warm kisses on her lips. She responded avidly and slipped her tongue into my mouth. Fred had lowered the lights—we were virtually in the dark. After a few minutes I decided to try the other hole. As I reached for the spot I felt something hard and hairy. A weak voice, mirthful too, called out *"It's me, Joey."* The three of us burst out laughing and disengaged.

Turning the lights up a bit we spontaneously decided that we would go at it in a natural, more comfortable way. My bedroom was next to the studio. We would have her one at a time. Ariadne smiled agreeably. The question was—who was to tackle her first?

Joey thought I should, since they were my guests. I saw no sense in standing on punctilio and so off Ariadne and I went to my double bed. As she didn't have much on it took no time to strip. She was beautifully built, a delight to all the senses. We hugged and kissed and caressed, did all manner of fool things, but for the life of me I could not get an erection. (Perhaps because it was all too *facile*.) Finally I gave up trying and called to Joey in the studio. He came in on the double trot.

I confessed that I was impotent and told him it was time to try his luck. He jumped into the bed immediately and was all over her.

However, in about ten minutes, I heard him calling for me. I went into the bedroom to find him lying dejectedly beside his Ariadne. He too had found himself impotent.

Instead of taking it tragically we all got dressed and went to the *Coupole* for drinks and a light snack. Ariadne took it like a brick. She said it was one of those things—it even happened to women sometimes. "By the way," she added, "Eugene will be back tomorrow. I had a letter from him today."

Two days later Fred appears at my place about eight in the morning—early for him. "Can I use your bathroom?" he said. "Of course," I replied, whereupon he loped off to the bathroom. He was hardly gone when there came a harsh knock at the door. I opened it and who do I see before me but Eugene. I started to say *"Bon jour!"* but he cut me short with—*"Où est-il?"* (Where is he?) I shrugged my shoulders, not realizing at first whom he was referring to. He pushed me roughly aside, walked through my bedroom and opened the bathroom door. There was Joey waiting for him and trembling no doubt. The first word out of Eugene's mouth was *"Salaud"* followed by what sounded like a slap in the puss. More epithets flowed from Eugene's lips, always followed by slaps or blows. Now I heard Eugene berate him for not defending himself. "Coward!" he yelled and then more bang bang. It sounded bad. I didn't dare go to Fred's rescue as I was due for some of that punishment myself—or had Ariadne only told on Fred and not me?

Anyway in a few minutes Eugene appeared, brushed by me without saying a word and disappeared. A few moments later Joey made his appearance, looking rather battered and bruised but with a grin on his face.

The first thing I said to him was—"How could you take a beating like that and not defend yourself?" He grinned some more, sheepishly this time, and replied: "I didn't try because I deserved what I got."

"You mean you kept your hands at your sides and let him make a punching bag of you?"

"Exactly," he said. "I was guilty. It was a lousy thing to do to a friend. I deserved every bit of it. I even feel good about it. Sort of soothes my conscience."

With that we dropped the matter. I even forgot to ask him where he was going to sleep hereafter. (I couldn't offer to put him up in my place because it would risk displeasing Anaïs.)

The more I mulled the matter over—I mean his refusal to defend himself—the more I had to admire him. We have all taken beatings at one time or another but rarely voluntarily. He was dead right too about the punishment soothing his conscience. There was one puzzling factor which was never resolved. Why had Ariadne told on Fred and not on me? Was it because the whole truth would have been too much for Eugene to take? Or was she endeavoring to preserve the friendship which Eugene and I had shared for years? One never really knows what motivates a woman's behavior. To men they always seem to have an affinity with cats. In a word they are "treacherous." Men are too, of course. But women seem to be born that way. Men only acquire it with growing experience of life. In a way there was also something feline about Joey himself. Women adored him, loved him, helped him, but usually sensed that at bottom he was not to be trusted. He amused them, flattered the pants off them and used them—and, for some inexplicable reason they did not mind too much. His continuous air of cajolery seemed to have a mollifying effect on them. Besides, it's no great secret that women are easy prey for rogues, liars, scoundrels. They may refuse to give themselves to the good and earnest man who reveres them, and allow themselves to be seduced by the first Romeo who comes along. Not only that, but at bottom their behavior is often far more shocking than that of men. A woman, for example, who passes for the incarnation of virtue may be discovered eventually to be a lascivious bitch—worse, an unacknowledged whore. She may have a vicious streak, demanding to be fucked only in certain ways, certain positions, all this, mind you, while playing the role of good wife and devoted mother. And sometimes, by Jesus, she really can be both things at once.

Of course there are plenty of men given to the same deceit and treachery, but usually they are not as artful as women. They betray themselves more readily. They are more insouciant.

Why is it that the man who has been made *"cocu"* (cuckold) always appears ridiculous to our eyes? Raimu, the famous French actor, played this role in its dual aspect marvelously. He was at once naive and ridiculous and then tragic in the real Shakespearean sense.

I don't think Fred ever suffered from a broken heart. Oh, perhaps yes, when he was still a youth, but not after he had matured. The trouble with him was that he was very silent, very reticent about his youth. It was almost as if he had never known such a period. He probably went from the university to the army and thence to the bughouse. It was here at the bughouse that I imagine him to have done his greatest reading. Trust the Germanic instinct for learning to have provided even their insane asylums with good reading matter. I feel almost positive it was there he got to know his Goethe—*Conversations with Eckermann. Dichtung und Wahrheit, The Italian Journey;* perhaps Faust too and Wilhelm Meister. When tipsy and acting the buffoon the line which often came to his lips was: *"Das ewige Weibliche zieht uns immer hinein."* He would mouth this famous phrase with the same mock solemnity that a Jesus freak might quote the Golden Rule.

He could also recite in this manner with one hand up his girl's dress, tickling her clitoris. Or he could recite it sitting on the toilet. There was something delicious about his pranks, his roguery. One hears of men who would betray their own mother if they badly needed a meal or a pair of new socks. What's more, the likes of them often are not at all detestable—on the contrary. That is why I return again and again to the congruity of the cat and the rogue. What to me is so despicable in the cat is the way it curries favor by rubbing itself against your leg, or purring so gently and softly—like wheedling a blind man out of a bit of cash.

With all his feline qualities I want to emphasize once again that whatever lousy thing Joey might do he remained a lovable guy, *a friend.* He could rob you barefacedly and with the other hand give you a caress. Perhaps there is a bit of truth in the Germans' reference to Austrians, especially Viennese, that they are "treacherous." One hears the same about the Italians, how they smile at you as they put a stiletto in your back. But they too, the Italians, are a lovable sort and are always forgiven their faults. Tourists (women especially) are fond of telling how awful the Italian men are, that they will pinch a woman's ass even if she is walking with her own husband. But once again one must bear in mind that women secretly enjoy being pinched in the ass, and especially in that sly way the Italians do it.

After *Tropic of Cancer* had been out a month or two there appeared a review of the book by none other than my favorite writer Blaise Cendrars. It came out in a little review called *Orbes*, run by one of Cendrars's most devout admirers. One day shortly after this happening Cendrars and his friend came unexpectedly to visit me at the Villa Seurat. To their dismay they saw posted on my door a printed, or rather handwritten sign reading—"Do not disturb! Genius at work." Cendrars took it good-naturedly and refused to disturb me but his friend to whom Cendrars was a god was highly incensed. He wanted to break the door down.

A week or two later Cendrars came alone. This time I responded quickly. Fred was in my place at the time. Again we were short on drinks and broke to boot. But no thought of any funny business. I explained the situation to Cendrars frankly, knowing he would understand. In any case we rationed the little that was left of the cognac and husbanded our tiny portions as best we could during a two or three hour session with Cendrars.

What a marvelous afternoon we spent together, talking of everything under the sun but mostly of his adventures in various parts of the world.

I recall now two things he mentioned which surprised me. One was his dislike of Marcel Proust's work and the other was his facination with or obsession with Rémy de Gourmont— both the man and his writing. He told of one strange incident that sticks in my crop. I believe he had just informed us that de

Gourmont was a leper and went out only at night. One evening as Cendrars was about to cross one of the famous Paris bridges he thought he recognized a figure bent over the parapet, gazing idly at his own image in the water below. He looked again and was certain now that it was one of two men he most admired at the time—the other being Gérard de Nerval. Yes, he was sure it was Rémy de Gourmont—he had seen enough photos of him to be certain.

Not wishing to obtrude upon his idol, Cendrars nonchalantly advanced a few steps until he was almost touching de Gourmont and then he too leaned over the parapet gazing into the Seine. He wanted badly to talk to de Gourmont but was too shy to introduce himself. So he began talking to his own image in the water, but about things which he knew would interest his idol and let him know he was talking about him. I believe he began by talking of some of the authors de Gourmont wrote about in his less well-known work about Latin authors. I don't remember whether de Gourmont responded in any way but at least he didn't move away. It was a characteristic gesture on the part of Cendrars. Rough adventurer that he was, he was also one of the gentlest, most sensitive men I ever met.

The afternoon wore on most agreeably, with Cendrars doing most of the talking whilst Fred and I listened open-mouthed and dumbstruck. Finally Cendrars announced that he was getting hungry, wouldn't we like to have dinner with him; he knew, he said, a wonderful modest restaurant in Montmartre near where Picasso and Max Jacob once had a studio. It was on the rue de l'Abbesse, if I am not mistaken.

To make it easier for us to accept his invitation he lied about having just that morning unexpectedly received a check from one of his publishers.

In the street around the corner from us was a cab rack. (Rue de la Tombe-Issoire.) The restaurant was indeed a cosy little joint with a bar which was already occupied from one end to another by a group of whores. Cendrars was well-known to the proprietor and to the girls also, it appeared. The first thing he did on taking our seats was to order *un coup de champagne pour les jeunes filles en fleurs* (mocking Proust) adding aloud, glass in hand, that these were France's true ambassadors. This immediately created a genial atmosphere.

When it came time to eat, Fred and I offered to cut his steak for him. He politely refused, saying the waiter was used to doing it for him. A few moments later he was to get up and stand in the show window to show us all how he could touch any part of his body with his sole left hand. (But not cut his own steak.) On the other hand it is well-known that he drove a Bugatti not only through the heavy traffic of Paris but up the Amazon. It was there among the head-hunters that he learned the trick of showing how he could reach any part of his body with just the left hand. He told us it had saved his life, as the natives (head-hunters) found this exploit highly amusing.

It was interesting to note how his familiarity with the whores at the bar did not alter his gentleness. This man, who had lost his good right arm as a *Légionnaire* was the same man who in answer to a questionaire—"What quality in women do you admire most?" wrote *"Innocence."*

Well, we had an excellent meal, probably cooked especially for him and his friends, washed down with his favorite wines. It was a royal feast and we, Fred and I, were slightly tipsy.

When Cendrars suggested that we now go bar-hopping (along the *grands boulevards de Montmartre*), Fred made some excuse and took leave of us. (He did this out of delicacy, not wishing to impose further on Cendrars's hospitality.) I *had* to go along with Cendrars because he considered me a genuine pal. Often during our conversations he would remark about the parallelism of our lives just before the First World War. He liked to remind me that he too had been a bum and a beggar in New York, that he hated work, that his one passion was reading, etc., etc.

So we began stopping off — a bar here, a bar there. Everywhere immediately recognized by the proprietor, bartenders and *clientèle*. Tough *hombre* that he was, I noticed he stuck to his white wine (usually *un* Meursault) rather than Pernods and cognacs.

At one bar where there was a cluster of whores at the counter he opened the blouse of the girl standing next to him, pulled out her planturous teat and turning to me said: *"Regarde-moi ca! C'est beau, n'est-ce pas?"* What he wanted me to observe closely were her lovely *"nichons"* (nipples) which were the color of grapes. All this in good fun, not with vulgar ostentation. The girls seemed to know him and respected him as a famous writer, though I doubt any had read him.

Toward four in the morning I managed to break away, saying (the truth!) that I had to go to the Central Post Office to deposit some mail which would just catch one of the fast ocean liners going to New York.

A memorable, an unforgettable evening. Never repeated, alas!

Well, back to *mon copain*, Alf, Joey, Fred. . . . *Les Dégourds du Onzième*, by Courteline. A book I often wanted to talk to Fred about but never did. There were certain authors both French and English, I never heard him mention. And yet he was extremely well-read. Which reminds me that there are two characters I have neglected to mention thus far—Hans Reichel, the painter, and Betty Ryan, the girl downstairs. It was one Christmas morning that both Reichel and Fred happened to visit me about the same time—early morning. Though none of us gave a damn about Xmas, nevertheless we felt the occasion warranted some modest sort of celebration. As so often happened there were just the dregs of a bottle of white wine available. All the empty bottles of the nights before were lined up like sentinels beside my desk. Nothing daunted, Reichel suggested we pour the remains of the wine bottle into three tiny glasses—like thimbles really. This we did, then toasted one another and, as we began to converse, did our best only to take the barest sip from our tiny glasses.

Somehow this procedure reminded Reichel of his days in a French concentration camp during the First World War. (He had had to flee Germany at a moment's notice because he was guilty of harboring the Communist playwright Ernst Toller.) Anyway, in the concentration camp, when the rations were scarce or nil, he would don an apron and pretend to be a waiter, going to each prisoner in turn and asking what he would like to eat. (He would first rattle off an imaginary menu which would make everyone's mouth water.) He repeated some of the antics he employed. Like Fred, he too was a good clown. We enjoyed his imitation immensely. From this he went on to talk of his friendship with Paul Klee, whose painting he was often accused of imitating. Anyone who knew both men's work intimately could never make this assertion. However, it now gave him pleasure to tell us in his inimitable way (using French, English and German) how very much alike the two of them were in many ways. In fact, as he put it, they were like brothers. As I recall it now, many years later, Reichel informed us that not only did they think and paint in similar fashion, but they both played the violin, and fell in love with two sisters, among other things. "How could we help but paint alike?" he added. "We were like twins."

Now it happened that just below me on the ground floor was a young lady, also a painter, who was an ardent admirer of Reichel's work. And Reichel, for his part, was an ardent admirer of the young woman. In fact, he was conducting a secret love affair with her. The young woman was not only highly sensitive and angelic but somewhat eccentric. She preferred the company of men to women.

One day she invited about fifteen or twenty of her men friends to a banquet downstairs in her quarters. In addition to a choice selection of wines she also offered us cognac, chartreuse and other cordials. The dinner was going along fabulously until Reichel took one drink too many, whereupon he changed as usual into a demonic, quarrelsome individual. Now Reichel had always suspected me of having designs on the young lady—and in truth he was not far off the mark. And so, in very blunt Germanic fashion he began talking sheer nonsense. Pointing to one of his treasured watercolors on the wall he said it meant nothing to him, that he could destroy it as easily as he had created it. For some crazy reason I was in a somewhat diabolical mood myself. And so I began to twit him. Finally, rising from my seat, I went to the painting in question, put my hand on it, and dared him to destroy it in front of us all. I really believed he was capable of doing this, but to my great surprise, he refused, and grabbing his full glass of wine smashed it against another wall. With this our hostess became positively alarmed. Reichel, seemingly humiliated, called for stronger drinks and began to curse and swear in German.

With this, several of the guests (Frenchmen) took their leave. And in a little while, one by one, they all bade their hostess goodnight and left. I was left alone with her. I saw that she was quite drunk and I wanted no part in what might follow. So in a moment I too said goodnight and started upstairs to my studio. The young lady was now not only indignant over the failure of her party but outraged. She picked up several half-empty glasses as I started up the stairs and flung them at me. I kept mounting the steps, never turning a head to look back at her. That positively enraged her. More glasses were hurled and smashed to smithereens against the stone steps.

For almost an hour all was quiet. I had gone to bed to take a nap. Suddenly I heard the young woman calling my name. I opened the door and there she was at the bottom of the stairs, making ready to come up.

"But the glass!" I shouted.

"I don't give a damn," came the reply.

And so, in bare feet over the broken glass she came up the flight of stairs with bloody feet.

Of course I washed her feet and did my best to staunch the flow of blood.

She was still in a sombre mood. "What ever got into you?" I asked.

"You!" she replied. "*You* egged Reichel on. You knew he was in love with me. You did it deliberately."

I could not deny the truth of this. All I could do was to bandage her feet and invite her to get in bed with me.

Will the reader kindly regard the foregoing about the broken glass as an interlude to the Christmas passacaglia which I am now about to continue. . . .

We left Reichel, Fred and myself slowly draining the thimblesful of cognac which Reichel had doled out in three equal portions.

During the conversation which took place all that morning—or rather "the reminiscences"—it occurred to me, as it had on previous occasions in which the past was celebrated that Fred never seemed to have had a youth or else had completely forgotten it—or it was simply lost in the night of history.

Whereas myself, not only on this occasion but often in my life I could recollect (and delighted to do so) many, many things out of my days from five to ten years of age in "the old neighborhood."

Back to that Christmas Day in 1930 something or other. The morning visitation—then a sleepy afternoon with Fred popping in again around four in the afternoon to see if by some miracle I had rustled up some food. "Sorry, Joey, but no luck. We'll just have to pull our belts tighter." But then in about an hour the miracle occurred. About 5:00 P.M. there was a rap at the door. I go to open it and there stands a charming couple—young man and woman of indeterminate age—just over from England. Hoping to spend part of Christmas Day with Henry Miller whose books they have devoured. I had barely introduced my pal Joey when it occurred to me to tell them the truth about our situation—that we were broke and not a morsel nor an ounce of liquor in the larder.

"Have you any money on you?" I asked bluntly.

Of course they had. They would be only too happy to go look for some food for us all.

What a godsend! We blessed them and told them where to look for the food.

When they returned about half an hour later they were laden

with good things—a roast chicken, vegetables, fruit, wines, liqueurs, cigarettes. They had thought of everything. The woman, whom I will call Pat, went to work immediately to prepare the dinner. The young man, who was an unknown writer, helped set the table, talking books all the while. I soon discovered that he was familiar with my own favorites— Cendrars, Max Jacob, et al, and the French painters, Braque, Matisse, Bonnard, et al.

Fred meanwhile was helping Pat prepare the food. They were having an animated conversation, it seemed. Later he told me that she had confided in him that she was a poet, "a little mad," and had only recently been released from the insane asylum. And British to boot!

We sat down to table in a little while and tackled the *hors d'oeurves*, which they had remembered to bring, including *céléri remoulade* (sic). At table we gradually learned who the young woman with the white hair was. She was a poetess, not known in every household in England but well-known in the halls of poesy and lunacy. At table the rapport between her and Fred (they sat opposite one another) was striking. I hardly ever had seen Fred in such a joyous and serene mood. He recited from French and German poets. She in turn quoted from her own work, which was excellent and extremely modern. Not crazy either. Rather a mixture of coolth and passion, restraint and abandon, immanence and permanence, nightly emissions, *asamara*, fragile jonquils. The wines they had brought were superb—chateau vintages no less. And with the dessert came the Armagnac, the chartreuse, etc. A royal feast, if ever I had one!

In the midst of it Pat suddenly gets up, goes round to Fred, and embraces him. A long, warm embrace. They were both reeling beside the table. Suddenly, without a word, Fred takes her by the arm, and leads her to my bedroom. There, as I later learned, he gave her a quick fuck—but, as he put it—a *good* one. In a few minutes they came out, looking perfectly nonchalant, and resumed their places at the table.

From here on until they left it was poetry and song. What I could not help but notice was the remarkable affinity between the two. Could it have been that her recent release from the asylum reminded Fred of his own four years in the nut house, as a casualty of the war?

Though there was probably no connection between the two events, it was a fact that not long after their meeting, Fred went to England to live, became a British citizen, and when the war began, enlisted in the British Pioneer Corps, as I believe it was called.

It was some half hour or so after they had gone, and we two were still sitting at the table. From where Fred sat he could see the window up above my balcony. It was a small window but large enough for any sized moon to shine through. Suddenly he glanced up at the window and let out a shriek. A three-quarter moon (on the wane) was mirrored in the little window. It was a cheesy looking moon, as if chunks had been bitten out of it.

Fred of course immediately jumped to his feet and moved to the other side of the room. He repeated what he had told me several times before—that the sight of the moon always unnerved him. He was very much like a woman in a tantrum. I offered him some more Armagnac but he decided he had had enough, grabbed his beret and left.

I was left with the garbage and the dirty dishes. The place was a mess. In my excitement I completely forgot that the *femme de menage* was due next morning and so, as I hustled about, cleaning up the mess, I began humming to myself and recalling scenes out of my early childhood, then scenes at the piano in my sweetheart's home, playing her favorite melodies. In retrospect I had risen from the piano stool, embraced her warmly, then run my hand up her dress and felt her warm, throbbing cunt. That was as far as I permitted myself to go. Suddenly at this point I thought of my old friends and acquaintances in the old neighborhood. "Merry Christmas! Mrs. Reynolds!" I shouted. "Merry Xmas Mr. Ramsay, you old goat! Merry Xmas Mr. Pirossa, may your bananas slowly ripen! Fuck Jesus! Fuck the Virgin Mary! Fuck Gautama the Buddha! Peace on Earth with neutron and hydrogen bombs! Vive the clap! Vive Syphilis the brother of Satan! When you are in love you must destroy right and left! Long live the street cleaners. Bless the uncteries! Long live Insanity! A new day is dawning, an even worse one. Run for your life! Take cover! Fuck your sister, your mother, your aunt, your cousin! Not a crumb of the past will be left. Not a morsel, not even a speck. A clean sweep. Pure, beautiful annihilation."

"Roses, roses, roses bring memories of you dear. . . ."

Fuck you all! The earth rejects you. Satan rejects you. The cherubim reject you. You are disappearing into nothingness and leaving not a shred of memory behind. You are not even so much horse shit! Ta ta!

During the war Fred and I corresponded. I learned that he intended to write a book about me, about our friendship. He intimated that he would like to visit me in Big Sur for a few months, if I could put him up conveniently. I was then married to Eve McClure. The children were down south staying with their mother and her new husband. They weren't too happy about the new arrangement. Tony, my son, took it especially hard. I used to telephone him once a week. I noticed that he answered in monosyllables—yes, no, maybe, etc. That made me feel wretched.

However, vacation time was soon due and then they were free to stay with Eve and me a few months.

Fred had already arrived and taken to the life immediately. I'll never forget the look of wonder and pleasure on his face when we took him to Monterey to shop. As usual we stopped for lunch at a lunch counter which served hamburgers. I don't think Fred had ever seen a hamburger before, much less eaten one. He wore that expression of glee which one sees on the faces of kids on TV when attempting to down a monstrous sandwich.

Eve, my wife, found Fred to be a darling. We had a Mexican, or rather Panamanian friend (female) who also took a great liking to Fred and offered him sexual satisfaction if he got hard up. Then there were the hot springs where we usually went once a week.

All in all, everything was just ducky.

Finally it came time to pick up my kids for their vacation. We were to meet at a bus station in Santa Maria, if I am not mistaken. I had an old beaten up jeep, which looked rather like a museum piece. Fred wanted to go with me. He had heard a lot about the children not only from Eve and myself but from the neighbors also. Everyone described them as "darling."

Fred seemed surprised that I could drive as well as I did. (I was always the most unhandy bugger imaginable.) But I learned to do many things living in the country which I never thought possible in New York or Paris.

Well, we arrived at the bus station and there, sitting placidly on a bench were my two kids with their mother and step-father. One could see at a glance that they had been scrubbed clean as a whistle, been arrayed in their best clothes and told to sit quietly until we arrived.

The moment I appeared they jumped from their seat and shouted and climbed all over me. "Daddy, daddy!" they yelled. They acted as if they had just been released from prison. I could see that Fred, who had never had anything to do with children, was already somewhat apprehensive.

Well, we quickly piled into the jeep, the kids occupying the rear seat, and started homeward. The moment I put my foot on the gas pedal and veered toward home pandemonium set in. They flung a hundred questions at me at once.

I glanced now and then in Fred's direction and thought I de-tected a look of growing terror on his face. Certainly the kids behaved as if uncontrollable—a pair of wild animals. (But *lova-ble* ones!) I of course was thrilled at this unexpected reception. I realized, without their saying a word, what a disciplined life they had been leading at their mother's house. And so I allowed them to carry on in their own sweet way. They sang, they yelled, they asked a thousand questions about their old (young) friends and so on. Sheer insanity. After driving a bit I noticed that it was getting dark and that we would have to stay at a motel and continue on in the morning.

I believe I chose Andersen's, a well-known hotel and restau-rant. We took one large room with three beds. First we had hamburgers and tea or coke. This revived their spirits and so, when we entered our room they went absolutely berserk. Fred gave me a look as if to say—"Can't you calm them down just a little bit?'' But I was so happy to see them in this joyous, if crazy mood, that I made no attempt to put the brakes on them. I didn't care if they ripped the place apart.

Naturally, there had to be a debate as to who would sleep with whom. I suggested that Tony and Val sleep together and Fred and I separately in our own beds. I think it was Tony who wanted to sleep with Fred or me. Not getting his way he began a pillow fight. Soon all four of us were throwing pillows at one another. I thought because of the pandemonium that the manager might order us to leave, but fortunately he let us be.

It must have taken a couple of hours before they were ready to sleep. I could see that Fred was already worn out. Our gambits in the Villa Seurat days were nothing compared to these shenanigans.

Well, next day we arrived home and received a warm greeting from Eve. She immediately set about preparing a beautiful lunch for us all.

Tony meanwhile had found some of his old toys and a big top hat (for the opera) which he donned and began his antics in the garden. It was curious to watch my son, a Virgo like Fred (born the same day of the month) act the clown which was Fred's forte. They definitely had something in common, though I don't think Fred was quite aware of it as yet. He regarded the "two monsters" as if they were freaks from the circus. He always kept a little distance between himself and them, much as Moricand had tried (unsuccessfully) to do with Val.

What a misfortune not to have children of one's own. Certainly they can create trouble but whatever the pain or discomfort it is worth having them. I only wish I had been able to produce a round dozen.

Well, Fred stayed on two, three or four months, and finished his book, *Mon Ami Henry Miller*, there in Big Sur. And what a beautiful, loving book it is! Written from the heart, if ever a book was thus written. No bullshit, no academic appraisals— just the simple, plain, natural truth.

I wind up this chapter about him with tears in my eyes. He was a friend indeed, an unforgettable one.

I wrote was instead of is. He is still alive and still living in England, only now he is living in Dorset (Thomas Hardy's country). My son, Tony, who has always had a secret admiration for Fred, intends to visit him sometime this year. This time Fred will not meet with a wild Indian but a handsome, intelligent young man who is a chip off the old block. May the two Virgos have a rollicking time of it.

Epilogue

Dear Joey,

As you probably know, Anaïs died a year or so ago. Before dying she left instructions for two of her very dear friends to republish the *Diaries* exactly as she wrote them, to translate into English the early childhood diaries, and to write a biography which would tell the whole truth about her life. All these things are now being done.

You may also know that an erotic books she had withheld until her death has been selling like wildfire. It's called *The Delta of Venus.*

One other little, but touching item. Before her death she wrote a letter to Hugo, her first husband, asking him to forgive her for all her "capers," her lies, the tricks she played behind his back; in short, for all her misdeeds as a wife, which, needless to say, were legion. To her delight and *soulagement* he told her that he had always loved her, that he was aware of her "shenanigans" (my word, not his) and that there was nothing to forgive.

All this made me recall how she treated *you*, how unforgiving she was. And you were only trying to let her and everyone know how much you loved her.

With her death she left behind a host of admirers and idolaters, mostly young women. How they will react when they learn the truth I cannot at this moment conceive. (In my own case, when I learned the truth about Knut Hamsun's behavior during the Second World War, it made no difference whatever in my feelings toward him. He still remains a hero to me.)

We (you, I, Durrell) knew about Anaïs's lying and deceit long, long ago. I mentioned earlier in this narrative about "falling out of her favor." You were not the only one to be dismissed, as it were. There were others. But what always stuck in my crop, Joey, was the utter unfairness of her behavior with you. And what, after all, was your crime? That you told the truth about her and her relationships. But you did it innocently, without malice. *That* she simply refused to see, unfortunately.

Anyway, before very long, the whole world will be made aware of her inveterate lying, her chicanery, her duplicity, and so on. I myself, who was perhaps her best friend, have referred to her as a monstrous liar or prevaricator or fabulator, however one feels like expressing it. I have discussed this aspect of her being with her most loyal, devoted female friends. We are all agreed that this inability to tell the truth was based on her inability to accept reality. She had to alter reality to suit her own view of the world. You may remember her abhorrence of vulgarity, that it was worse than sin to her. (I have mentioned in this narrative that she was not ever present during our "orgies," so to speak.) And it was this compulsion of hers which drove her to write her *Diary*. In it one is tempted to say— everything was upside down.

And now I come to the point of this long detour, which is— why not get out your original manuscript about her and seek a publisher for it. After all, it is not a piece of gossip but an adoring tribute to her. Yes, Joey, a "loving portrait," far better than what I have done for you.

Now is the time. Her *Delta of Venus* was on the best seller list for a number of weeks. How ironical that she who detested "vulgarity" should win posthumous fame by a highly erotic work!

Unfortunately, I only remember the flavor of that book you

devoted to the super-terrestrial aspect of her being. In those days I used to say to myself (mockingly), "Joey is good at that sort of thing." You were indeed far closer to understanding her very special nature than I who was her intimate friend. Many times, as I look back on those years, I can see again the expression on your face which told me what a brash, insensitive American I was. Often this would happen when I would question you about some famous old German writer whose name I happened to run across. You would simply say "He's not for *you*, Joey," and that was all. But you cannot realize how crushing those simple rejoinders were. It told me not only that I was Brooklyn born, without a real education, and that, like most Americans, I know little or nothing about Europe, but that, try as I may, I would never have the insight, the sensitivity that most Europeans are blessed with. How right you were! Arriving in Paris a whole new world confronted me—language, literature, culture, social behavior, eating habits, just about everything. And Anaïs, though born in France, never really understood or appreciated her native land as did you, a foreigner like myself. It was not with Anaïs but with *you* (and with Larry too) I held lengthy discussions about French authors, French habits, French streets and so on. Anaïs, who was quite a reader, always seemed to skim the surface.

In a profound sense she lacked a religious instinct. Having renounced Catholicism she closed the door on all mysteries. Yet, in spite of her faults and shortcomings she remained in our eyes a creature not of this world, nor of the heavenly world, but someone floating felicitously between Heaven and Earth. She was forever ethereal, forever guileless, forever innocent. And withal a helper, a sort of Mother Earth. She could no more shut her eyes to distress than she could to vulgarity. If she sinned, and God only knows how she did, it was as a child, a child who had not yet opened her eyes on the world.

And Joey, my dear, my abiding friend, *you* knew all this better than anyone. In my crass American way I used to think of your writing then (particularly about Anaïs) as so much "embroidery." "He's good at that sort of thing." When, however, you came to write *Sentiments Limitrophes* and *Le Quatuor en Ré Majeur*, I began to realize whom I was living with, what a truly wonderful view of life you possessed. I would give anything to be able to reread those books now.

Although throughout this book I may seem to have dwelt more on your "scabrous" behavior, your perpetual clowning and deviltry, I am sure you know that, just as Anaïs floated between Heaven and Earth, so you always hovered between the clown and the angel. Perhaps "idiot" would be better suited to express what I tried to convey. Of course, I mean "Idiot" in the Dostoievskian sense and not as our born idiots take the word to mean. The older I grow the more meaningful and beloved that word has come to be for me. So, Joey, as one idiot to another, farewell for the time being. May you continue to live your happy-go-lucky life right to the end. You have brought laughter and tears to us all. Bless you,

Henry

POSTSCRIPT

One other little item remains to be touched upon. Strangely enough, you and Anaïs had this whatever you may call it in common. I mean a seeming lack of childhood. An absence of childhood friends. Try as I may, I cannot recall either of you dwelling on early friendships. Whereas in my own case, the years from five to ten seem now more than ever to have been the most important, the most wonderful years of my life. Furthermore, it is hard for me to imagine a childhood without friends. Even a doll or a wooden horse is something to remember in later years, something endearing.

But no, with both of you there existed this vaccuum. I am not going to try to analyze this lack or gap—that is for the psychologist to do, if he can. There is only one little trait you both shared which I will dare to mention—a need for secrecy. Often I felt that neither of you had anything to hide or to be ashamed of, but that you simply did not wish to share *everything* with even the best of friends.

I am probably all wrong, but I thought I ought to give voice to my suspicions. It doesn't alter my feelings about you; it simply makes you more "mysterious," closer to the angel than to the clown. *You* were the one who believed in miracles, remember? I can still hear you saying to me:—"Don't worry, Joey, something will turn up." And, by crickey, something usually did. I used to attribute this gift of yours to some sort of spiritual legerdemain which you carried with you from infancy, from a world I knew nothing about. Which reminds me now how farcical must have seemed my attitude of perpetually baring my soul. Do you remember the little story I once told you about going to a woman, a Jewish woman, who was a psychic individual? I had hardly crossed her threshold when she exclaimed "My good man, what have you done with your soul?" I instinctively felt in the neighborhood of my heart, where we imagine as children, the soul is located, and thought to myself—"She's so right, I must have lost my soul a long time ago." But enough of this. I feel now we shall meet again in the next world whenever and wherever.

OTHER WOMEN IN MY LIFE

Preface

A few days ago I had a birthday—my 86th. I had thought that I would do very little further writing, if any at all.

But two disparate occurrences in the last few days threaten to alter this decision, at least for one more book. The first factor was the absence of a fairly large sheet of watercolor paper which had been resting on the piano. It had been there for a couple of weeks and suddenly it was gone. On it, scribbled in helter-skelter fashion, were the names of almost all the women who had played some part in my life. I recall telling my son Tony, who had accidentally discovered this sheet, to take good care of it. Not that I then thought of writing about all these creatures.

The second factor was a remark by Simenon in his book *When I Was Old*. He stated that he was not a writer (regrettably) but a novelist and that being a novelist produced pain rather than ecstasy. This remark stuck in my crop. I asked myself how I would categorize myself. And immediately concluded that I was definitely not a novelist. Good or bad, from the very beginning of my literary career I thought of myself as a writer, a very important writer to be. I had no use for fiction, though many of my readers regard my work as being largely fictive. I myself am at a loss to give it a name.

But to come back to the women whose Christian names I used to cover a sheet of Arches watercolor paper. For some reason unknown to me I now have the urge to write about them. I may not use their right names, nor do I promise to be totally truthful or accurate in what I shall say about them. Rather, I prefer to think of them as Proust so aptly entitled his one volume — *Les Jeunes Filles en Fleur*. Scott Moncrieff, Proust's translator, named the volume *Within a Budding Grove*, which was nothing less than a stroke of genius.

My main motive in writing about these women is to evoke the aura of the times in which they lived. I will not pretend to give their life story, but only the essence and the fragrance of them as I sensed these at the time. Also, I shall not pretend that I slept with them all. On this score Simenon would seem to have broken all records. Much as I have dwelt on the sexual aspect of my relations with women in my previous work I must nevertheless now state that there were many other aspects in all the women I have known than what I chose to write about. Woman, as a subject, is endless. Like everything else, the skeptic may say. But in my humble opinion there is even more to her than the infinitude of sex would indicate.

PAULINE

Pauline was my first mistress. I met her while giving piano lessons. It was at the home of a friend of hers whose daughter was taking lessons from me—at thirty-five cents an hour. I was still madly in love with my first love, Una Gifford. I was teaching the piano in order to supplement my meagre salary working as a clerk for the Atlas Portland Cement Co. On my way home after giving a lesson I would stop off at an ice cream parlor near my home and eat two banana splits. They cost me thirty cents. The nickel that was left over I often threw in the gutter out of sheer disgust. I preferred to dig into my mother's purse for carfare next morning. One can see what little sense of reality I had.

But to come back to Pauline. She was usually seated in a chair some distance from the piano. Always neatly groomed, as if ready to go to the theatre or a concert. Hair always beautifully arranged and a pleasant smile on her face. Her friend, the mother of the girl I was teaching, was on the other hand something of a slut, careless about her apparel or her make-up. What the two women had in common was hard for me to tell.

To begin with, Pauline was from a small town in Virginia. She had a most pleasing Southern accent. Louise, her friend,

could have been from anywhere or nowhere. Louise had a
boarder, a black man, whose mistress she soon became. I knew
him as the man who ran the bicycle shop where I took my bike
to be repaired. But I was not aware immediately of the relationship between the two. That I discovered later from
Pauline.

Pauline had taken to calling me Harry. She thought Henry
too nondescript. We didn't fall into each other's arms immediately, I must confess. In fact, it *seemed* as if I were likely
to fall for her friend first. Louise was a lascivious bitch who
could hardly wait for the lesson to be finished before throwing
herself at me.

(Both women were in their thirties—I was eighteen.)
Another fact I discovered later about Louise was that she had
syphilis. That helped to resist her advances.

Usually, when the lesson was over, I escorted Pauline to her
flat. She was poor as a churchmouse but kept a neat, cosy flat
for which she paid a reduced rent in return for acting as jani-
tress. She had a son by a divorced husband who had been a
musician in the army. (She always referred to him as
"Shooter"—his last name, which was spelled "Chouteau.")
Her son George was just a year younger than I and worked as a
shoe salesman. He had a light tenor voice, very agreeable. He
and his mother often sang softly together—under their breath,
so to speak. Alone, especially doing her housework, Pauline
usually hummed to herself, something I found enchanting.
(I've only known one woman since who sang and hummed.)

From the foregoing it's obvious that I was now living with
Pauline. (And still madly in love with my first love.) I was
supposed to have gone to Cornell University but at the last
minute my father decided he could not afford to send me to

Cornell, even though I had been granted a scholarship in German. I had elected instead to take a job—at $30 a month. Naturally, these nightly walks past my true love's home were seriously curtailed.

Once during this period I ran into her by accident one evening at Coney Island. A most embarrassing moment, as Pauline was hanging on my arm. On another occasion, after moving to another flat, I discovered through a friend that my Una Gifford lived now in the house facing ours—and was married. I said nothing to Pauline about this, but now and then she would catch me looking through the window facing her yard with a dreamy expression on my face.

During this whole crazy adolescence I kept myself in good shape physically. I smoked a cigarette or two when I went to a party and drank wine when I went to an Italian restaurant, which was rather rare. No hard liquor. Lots of physical exercise. As I have explained elsewhere, for a good long time I virtually lived on my bike. In addition, I would run 3, 4, or 5 miles before breakfast. Before I took to living with Pauline I used to pass her flat every morning on my way back from Coney Island. She would be on the stoop waiting to see me pass. All we did was wave to one another. But that evening, after dinner, I was sure to be at her place, rearing to get my end in. Though she was old enough to be my mother—she had given birth to her son at the age of fourteen or fifteen—what a difference there was between the two women! Pauline was delicate, petite, beautifully proportioned, always of a cheerful nature. Uneducated but not stupid. In fact, her lack of schooling rendered her even more charming to me. She had taste, discretion, and a sound understanding of life. As I said before, she had not fallen for me at first blush. I believe she sensed what she was letting herself in for. She must have known from the beginning that it would end tragically for her. I, on the other hand, acted as if I were blind, deaf and dumb. I questioned nothing. I never looked ahead a millimeter. Of course it was my initiation into the world of sex. And it was a most beautiful one. As for Pauline, I am certain she had been deprived of a sex life for a number of years. She had never remarried and, so far as I knew, had had no lovers. We were both hungry for it. We fucked our heads off.

There was a strange interlude during which she met with an unexpected rival. It was the piano. I had given up teaching the piano and decided to become more proficient at it myself. I rented a piano — it cost almost nothing then — and took to practising at her place. She would lie abed waiting for me to quit. She was pregnant at the time, I remember, and probably needed much more attention than I gave her. Gone were the winter evenings when we sat by the kitchen stove, she in my lap, and fucked and fucked. We would take to bed and sleep before midnight. George, her son, was due home around midnight. We could always hear his footsteps as he mounted the stairs. When we did I would slide further down in the bed so that George would not notice me when he bent over his mother to kiss her good-night. Actually he must have surmised that I was in there with her, but he never let on.

In the Cement Co., where I was still working, I had an idol named Ray Wetzler. He lived at the N.Y. Athletic Club and was something of an athlete. I revered the ground he walked on. Often he would question me about my sporting life and about "the widow," as I called her. He took an unusual interest in me, not because I was such a good worker—I wasn't at all!—but because I was a rum bird, utterly unlike my fellow workers. Once, when the Xerxes Society, of which I was a member, rented a hall to give a dance, I invited Ray Wetzler to come—expressly to meet Pauline. The next day I was ravished when he told me she was beautiful and didn't look her age. He liked her Southern accent as well as her figure.

So, there I was at twenty-one. An athelete of sorts, a pianist, an utter romantic, starving, and tasting sex to the full. (At the time I believed I was in love with her.) She adored me, that I am positive of. Under the skin I was a Puritan. I felt guilty— imagine it!—for screwing this woman old enough to be my mother. One day I broached the subject of marriage. She didn't take to it very kindly. She tried to point out to me the absurdity of it, above all, that it would never work. But I was oblivious to her arguments. I decided that I would broach the subject to my mother—which shows what a naïve idiot I was.

I remember that I was sitting at the kitchen table. My mother was busy preparing a roast for dinner. She had a big carving knife in her hand. I had hardly got the words out of my mouth when she leaped toward me brandishing the big knife. "Not another word out of you," she screamed, "or I'll plunge this into your heart."

I made no attempt to answer back. I knew my mother—knew she was capable of anything when enraged.

When I recounted the incident to Pauline she said very simply, "I knew it wouldn't work, Harry, I know what your mother thinks of me. It's too bad." And with that we dropped the subject.

Meanwhile the pregnancy was becoming a matter of concern. Pauline was letting the months slip by, not from carelessness but from inability to have someone perform an abortion. There was also the question of money. (Always the question of money.)

I was still holding my job at the Cement Co. I hadn't received a raise, nor did I expect any. Married men with children were not earning any more than I at the time.

One day on coming home from work, I found her lying athwart the bed with legs dangling over the side of the bed. She was deathly pale and there were blood stains on the bed and on the floor.

I knelt over her and asked—"What happened?" She motioned weakly with her hand and in a very weak voice said: "Look in the bureau drawer."

I rushed to the bureau, opened the second drawer and there I saw the body of a child wrapped in a towel. I spread the towel and beheld a perfectly formed little boy, red as an Indian. It was my son. I choked on the realization of that fact. And from that to tears at the thought of what she must have suffered. It seems to be the lot of women to suffer. For the pleasures of the flesh they offer us men, we give them in return only pain. If the abortion itself was a horror the aftermath was even worse. The question was how and where to get rid of the body. The doctor, whoever he was—I never saw him—decided to chop the body into pieces and throw the pieces down the toilet. Naturally the toilet got clogged—and the landlady discovered all. She was not only irate but shocked and threatened to notify the police. How Pauline talked her out of doing this I don't know, but the result was that we were obliged to move on short notice.

Oddly enough, I never found out who the doctor was. I began to suspect that Michael, the man whom Pauline paid every week for the loans he made her, had had a hand in it.

How else was she able to get the money required for an abortion, done in one's home? Michael kept his accounts in a little book. He was very cordial, very affable, and always willing to advance more money, if needed. What Pauline paid him was a trifle—never more than a dollar, it seemed to me. I doubt if such a system exists today, unless it be among the blacks and the Mexicans. But as I have often said, the poverty of poor whites has always been unbelievable in this land of plenty.

I spoke of the piano being a threat to Pauline's love life. Even more were the books I was constantly reading. She was thoroughly mystified not only by the size of the books I brought home but by the quantity I devoured.

"What good is all that reading going to do you?" she would ask. And I would shake my head and reply—"I don't know, I just like to read." In those days there was neither radio nor television. Occasionally we would go to the movies, the *silent* movies, which cost about a dime then. What wonderful movies we saw, what great actors!

Coming home we had to climb two flights of stairs to reach our flat. I shall never forget the joy it gave me to follow behind her and goose her. As I stroked her she began to whinny, like a horse. The moment we opened the door to our flat we were in the kitchen and the kitchen table was waiting for us. She would lie on the table with her legs around my neck and I would sock it in like a monomaniac. I don't know any woman but one who enjoyed sex more than Pauline—and in a very natural way. She always seemed to be in a good mood, laughing and joking, during these bouts. No neurotic problems, no intellectual problems. "Easy does it."

To eke out an existence we finally took in a boarder. He was from Texas and worked as a motorman on a street car. He was a huge, pleasant, simple-minded individual with whom we had no trouble getting along. All he demanded was his round steak and fried potatoes and a bed to sleep in.

On the floor below us lived a married couple we saw quite a bit of. They were middle-aged. He was Lou Jacobs and she was Lottie. She was an inveterate cigarette smoker and he a pipe smoker. I was strongly attracted to Lou Jacobs for several reasons. First of all, he was like a father to me; second, he was a great reader, a reader only of great books; and last but not least he had a wonderful, if sardonic, sense of humor. He was such a person as I imagined Ambrose Bierce to have been. Cynical but kind, sardonic and religious, he was a philosopher and teacher both. Many were the authors we discussed when we were not playing chess. Like Marcel Duchamp, he was a fantastically good player, who did not play according to the rules but by instinct and intuition. With him as with Rene Crevel, "no daring was fatal." He would give me all manner of pieces, except of course his queen. He would often open a game by advancing a pawn on the rook's file. He was thoroughly unpredictable. Apparently he and his wife had had some tragic misunderstanding some years ago—I believe he had caught her in bed with their chauffeur. As punishment he never again made love to her. He treated her in a super-polite (mock) manner, as if she were the queen of the earth, but he wouldn't touch her. She seemed to have a great respect for him, despite his cruel treatment of her. As for Pauline, his manner toward her was always one of great deference, admiration and sympathy. He thought her beautiful and very feminine. (I often wondered later what their astrological signs were. In those days one heard very little of astrology.)

From some people you learn this, from others you learn that. From Lou Jacobs I learned many things.

I had been going with Pauline for almost three years now. Soon it would be my 21st birthday. And soon America would enter the First World War. I was still a faithful member of the Xerxes Society and still in love with Una Gifford. (In fact I've never gotten over it.) More and more my pals would poke fun at me for going with "the widow." Little did they know the delights an older woman can offer a young man. For not only was Pauline my mistress, she was also my mother, my teacher, my nurse, my companion, everything rolled into one. Though my companions felt she was much too old for me, Lou Jacobs didn't, nor Tex the motorman, nor Ray Wetzler, my idol.

Just before August 1914, an old buddy of mine, Joe O'Regan, happened on the scene. As usual, he came with some dough he had accumulated during his last job. Joe, incidentally, didn't find Pauline too old either. In fact, he took a shine to her from the start. It was a godsend of course that Joe had happened along when he did. The money which he handed over to me was no mean sum; it meant we could eat porterhouse once in awhile instead of plain round steak. For awhile all was ducky, we got along together, all of us, fine and dandy. But Joe, who was always horny, began making advances to Pauline in my absence. One day I came home to find her with tears in her eyes. Joe had been after her again. "I know you're his best friend," she began. "He idolizes you. But he should show more respect to me. He shouldn't try to betray his best friend."

I did my best to make excuses for Joe. I knew him to the ground. He would fuck his own sister if given the chance. He was just made that way. But he was also a lovable, generous guy.

One day came the news that war had broken out. (We had yet to join the holocaust.) The war seemed to change everyone's life, even ours though we were not yet participants. Everything became more serious, more stern and drastic.

I forget exactly how or why Joe disappeared, but he did eventually. Anyway, I had now made the acquaintance of an oculist who believed one could dispense with glasses if one exercised the eyes and led an outdoor life. Because of his talk I got the notion to give up everything and go West, become a cowboy. It was a lousy, a mean thing to do, but I left Pauline without telling her a word of my intentions. I believe I wrote her from the Garden of the Gods in Colorado, explaining things as best I could.

Needless to say, I never became a cowboy. I found a job on a lemon ranch in Chula Vista, California, where I threw dead branches on a fire all day long. I never rode a horse—at best I drove a sled harnessed to a jackass.

After a few months of this drudge work I decided to return to Brooklyn. The decision was made imperative through a chance meeting with Emma Goldman, the anarchist. It happened in this fashion. One night a cowboy friend at the ranch said he was going to town (San Diego) to visit a whorehouse he knew. He asked if I cared to go along and I agreed.

When we arrived in San Diego the first thing I espied was a huge poster announcing that Emma Goldman was lecturing that very night on European authors of renown. That decided it for me. I told my friend I would go to the whorehouse some other time.

It was a world-shaking event for me to hear Emma Goldman talk of the writers I so greatly admired—Nietzsche, Tolstoi, Gorky, Strindberg, et al. It changed the whole course of my life.

I left the lecture happy in the knowledge that I was not to be a cowboy but a man of letters.

But how to return home without losing face? Finally I hit upon an idea. I wrote Pauline to send a telegram to my folks, as if from California, saying "Sorry to hear of mother's illness. Leaving immediately. Signed Henry."

My mother of course was not fooled by the telegram. It was she who met me at the gate, with a look in her eye that told me everything.

For awhile I lived at home again, but visited Pauline every night and often stayed the night with her.

She was the same as ever. Her son George had died while I was away—of tuberculosis. I think Tex the motorman had left too.

Though everything was just the same, as I said a moment ago, still it was not the same. More and more I realized that I must break the tie. I no longer thought of Una Gifford, only of being free. What helped was that I had met the woman who was to become my first wife. She was my piano teacher.

I was going with her a few months when finally America joined the Allies against the Kaiser. I had left Pauline again, this time for good—and again without any explanation. A despicable thing to do, as I realized later, but typical of me at that time and even later.

One morning I awoke in bed with my piano teacher and it dawned on me with a rush that I might possibly be drafted for the bloody war. That was the last thing on earth I wanted to happen. I sprang out of bed shouting "We've got to get married!" and off I rushed to the barber for a shave and haircut. We were married in jig time and I felt fairly secure of not going to war.

It was a misalliance from the start. Constant bickering and

quarreling. I missed the harmony and serenity of my days with Pauline.

One night, as I was taking a stroll all by myself, I came across a cinema in which they were showing a foreign film I very much wanted to see.

I pushed the door open to go in and whom did I see standing in front of me with a flashlight but Pauline.

"Harry!" she cried and dragged me inside. She was weeping. She escorted me to a vacant seat and in a minute or two she joined me.

The tears were now streaming down her face.

"How could you do that to me?" she kept repeating.

I mumbled a few inanities, too moved to say much. I felt deeply guilty, deeply penitent. I had no excuse of any kind to offer. Escorting her to her new abode, where she worked as a maid, I managed to explain that I had married since leaving her. This brought on fresh tears, fresh sobs.

I was so distraught on leaving her that on the way home I decided I would invite Pauline to live with us. Why not? She had been a ministering angel to me. Why could I not reciprocate?

I could hardly wait to break the news to my wife. I might have known what a reception she would give my naïve suggestion. She not only treated it with ridicule (as who wouldn't?) but she made me out to be not only an idiot but a philanderer. In her mind I had invented this story of meeting Pauline in the cinema. She suspected I had been seeing her while I was "courting" her. (sic)

Despite the irony of the situation I kept on pleading with her. To soften my proposal I assured her I had no intention of sleeping with Pauline. I just wanted to offer her shelter and a bit of human kindness. I found myself talking to a stone wall. I became bitter and rancorous. I never forgave her for her "cruelty," as I called it. But that did no good for Pauline. I felt so ashamed of my failure to retrieve the situation that I never looked her up, never phoned her, never saw her again.

I have often wondered how she ended her days, for certainly she could not have lasted this long. I hope that Fate was kind to her.

That I was a son-of-a-bitch of the first water there is no doubt. Perhaps some of the ills I suffered since that time were meant as punishment for my behavior.

The worst of it all is that her good influence affected me not at all in my succeeding marriages. I was not made for marriage, that seems obvious. I was born to be a creative individual, a writer, no less, God save the mark. The only lesson I have learned in all these affairs is that an artist should never marry.

MIRIAM PAINTER

Miriam was her Christian name. Miriam Painter. I thought it a beatiful name then, about 75 years ago, and I still think so today.

We used to get out of school about the same time everyday—different schools but not far apart. Hers was on Moffatt St. and Evergreen Avenue and mine on Covert St. and Evergreen Avenue. Her way home obliged her to turn up my street—Decatur St.—which meant that soon we were walking and talking parallel to one another, she on one side of the street, I on the other.

She was somewhat like a faun; she had a loping gait which obliged me to maintain a steady trot to keep pace with her.

We only walked this way about one long block, from Evergreen Avenue to Bushwick Avenue. There she made an abrupt turn and we waved good-bye to each other.

Our conversation from one sidewalk to the other was never of any consequence. I haven't the slightest recollection of its content today, all I recall is her natural ebullience, her charm, her gaiety *and* what I took to be a special interest in *me*.

The fact that she was three or four years older than I was flattering to me. The other girls her age weren't near as friendly or, if I may put it that way, as approachable.

Having seen and talked with her the day was made for me. It was like a certain famous musician, Pablo Casals, who after his walk each morning sat down to the piano to play some Bach. That set *him* up for the day.

There were girls my age whom I knew and played with but by comparison with Miriam Painter they seemed coarse and vulgar. Miriam was destined to be "a lady," I was certain of it. Perhaps it was this factor which kept our daily intercourse the width of my street. We never touched, never kissed—only sidewalk to sidewalk.

She has remained in my memory for about seventy-five years now. Her name sounds just as beautiful today as the first time I heard it. It was not a prolonged friendship either. I would say it lasted a year or two at most. Nor was it an infatuation which possessed me, as did so often later. No, it was more like a scene on the stage. She simply went through a door that led nowhere and never returned. As I said a moment ago, I was in love with her (or her image) but not infatuated. Everything was delightful and yet of no great import. That's what I think now. But, am I not deceiving myself? Was there not something very significant in this seemingly trivial relationship?

Could it have been that it was my introduction to the enchanting nature of the female? It seems that all through my life women have played a dual role. Usually an affair would begin by being good friends. Later sex would enter and then there was the devil to pay. But almost always my loves have begun with a fragrance, with the simple seductiveness of creatures from another world. An instinctive reaction. I never knew much in advance of the woman who would later drive me mad.

If my memory serves me right there was at that time on the

New York stage a woman named Painter—or could it have been Fay Bainter? That may have contributed to making her name so attractive. At the corner of Decatur St. and Bushwick Avenue there was a rather large vacant lot. It was surrounded by a high fence on which large billboards advertising theatrical and musical stars frequently appeared. Sometimes just the title of the play stuck in my crop for years, like *Rebecca of Sunnybrook Farm*, which I never did see. Or it might be the name of a great singer, like Madame Schumann-Heink or Mary Garden. Or Laurette Taylor or Nazimova.

For some reason their names alone were magical. Certainly they were never talked about at home nor by my chums in the street.

What's in a name? you may ask. And I answer, *"Everything!"*

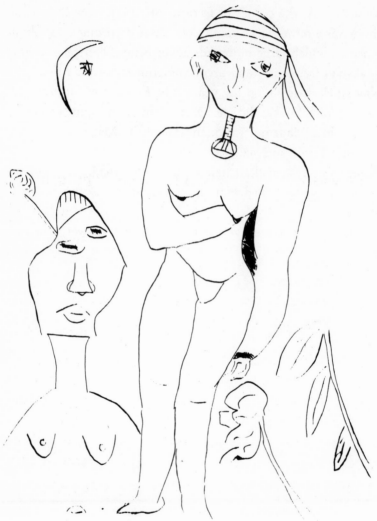

Epreuve d'Artiste — Jeune Fille — Henry Miller. 1973

MARCELLA

She was related to me in some way, probably as a second cousin. We got to know each other when we were in our teens. Usually we met on holidays or birthdays at one of the relatives' homes.

I had been playing the piano for five or six years and wherever I went where there was a piano I carried a roll of sheet music with me. The music I carried around was of two sorts— popular songs and classical music, such as Grieg, Rachmaninoff and Liszt.

Marcella, who was usually present at the festivities, thought I played beautifully. She had a good voice and was familiar with all the songs in my music roll. She was gay, buoyant, thoroughly alive.

One day I asked her if I could take her to a movie—in Manhattan. She readily accepted. Returning to her home we stood in the vestibule a few minutes kissing and hugging. As we did so I mumbled, "You know, Marcella, I think I am falling in love with you."

It was shortly after this I ran across the widow and had an affair which lasted a few years. No more family reunions, no birthday celebrations any more. I had definitely cut with all that nonsense. And of course I completely forgot about Marcella.

Through one of my relatives I learned that she had taken up with a boorish chap who sold cars. Apparently they didn't get along together very well. And, so I was told, Marcella had changed considerably in the interim. For one thing she had taken to drink. And it seems that now and then she drank so heavily that she passed out. Another strange thing was that she continued to go with this nobody but never got married—and she had been brought up a strict Catholic.

So, from time to time, I got rumors of her doings. Always surprising and always unpleasant or disheartening. Since we traveled in totally different circles we never had a confrontation. Not since that evening I had taken her to the movies— long ago.

Then suddenly a death occurred in the family and who attended the funeral but Marcella. She had changed greatly over the years. She looked heavier, coarser, somewhat sluttish.

It was after we had left the cemetery and gone to a beer garden for refreshments and drink that I managed to corner Marcella alone for a few moments.

I went up to her, greeted her warmly and asked in all innocence whatever in the world had come over her to change so.

To my utter astonishment she calmly replied, "*You!* It's all *your* fault!"

"Me," I echoed. "How do you mean?"

"You told me once that you loved me and I believed you."

"And so?"

"I kept waiting for you!"

"You kept waiting all these years without ever letting me know?"

She nodded.

"And so that's why you took to drink?"

She nodded again.

"That's downright stupid!" I exclaimed. She burst into tears.

I added: "You know, Marcella, ignorance is forgivable, but not stupidity." And with that off my chest I turned on my heel and walked off.

About a year later I learned that she had died—in the county hospital. She had become a hopeless alcoholic.

Silently I mumbled to myself—"And it was all your fault, Mr. Henry. Be careful next time you say '*I love you*' to anyone."

CAMILLA

Her full name was Camilla Euphrosnia Fedrant. She had black blood in her veins, or should I say white blood? I thought of her as a mulatto, a term one doesn't hear anymore for people of mixed blood.

At the time I was the employment manager of the Messenger Department of the Western Union Telegraph Company in New York City. Camilla was my assistant. How she got this job I have completely forgotten. I *believe* that she had appealed to the president of the Telegraph Company. She had excellent qualifications—a college graduate and of a very good college, a refined manner, quick on the trigger and very good-looking. In addition a good talker.

She sat opposite me at a double desk. Often, when I had finished hiring for the day, I would just sit and chat with her. She was a most intelligent young lady who really had no need for the excellent college education she received.

Shortly after she became my assistant we began hiring women to deliver telegrams in the tall buildings in which a Western Union office was usually located on the ground floor. The management thought this would lend an added touch. There was no feminist movement behind the innovation.

One day Camilla said to me, "Mr. Miller, I think some of these women messengers are getting out of line. I have received a number of complaints from our clients."

"What are you getting at?" I asked.

"I mean, to put it bluntly," said Camilla, "that some of these women have taken the job to ply their trade—prostitution."

To my surprise I found myself saying, "I can't blame them. If I were in their place I might do the same thing. You know this is considered to be about the lowest job on earth."

To this she replied, "I can think of lower ones—dishwasher, garbage collector and so on. I am not condemning these girls, or women, but I think Mr. So-and-so (meaning the general manager) ought to be informed."

I disputed this. I went on to tell her how in the old employment office, I used to pretend to offer a woman a job and then screw her after hours in the clothing department.

"I think you were a cad," she said calmly, somewhat surprised by my easy sense of morality. She knew, on the other hand, how many boys I helped out of my own pocket. She knew that they venerated me and came to me with their problems.

"Don't let's talk about it anymore," I said. "How about having dinner with me tonight?" She readily agreed. We had been doing this for some time now. Usually I picked a cozy little joint in the Village where there was a dance floor and perhaps a trio of musicians. Between courses we would dance, if you could call it that. Actually what we were doing was having a dry fuck, as they called it. Camilla was what we would call "sexy" today. (I thought of her as a lascivious bitch.) I never knew exactly where she hailed from but surmised it was from

Cuba or somewhere in the West Indies. I mentioned that she was a mulatto. She was so pale that she could pass for white. Besides her pale skin there was her speech and her deportment which was far superior to that of the American white woman, even the well-educated ones.

If it was a pleasure to dance with her it was even more of a pleasure to converse with her. She was extremely well-read, not only in English, but in Spanish and French. I think she secretly felt that she had the makings of a writer in her.

Among the youngsters I hired and with some of whom I was on rather intimate terms was a chap called Blackie. He was fifteen or sixteen, handsome, intelligent, and somewhat ahead of his years. Without my telling him he guessed that I was rather fond of my assistant. One day he took me aside to tell me he had some interesting news for me. Just how it began I have forgotten. But in some bizarre way he had made the acquaintance of Camilla's girl friend, a white aristocrat from New England. And he had put the boots to her, young as he was. She was in her early thirties. He ended the story by wondering aloud if they could possibly be lesbians.

I noticed that Camilla did not show any liking for my little friend and so I never broached the subject to her.

It hadn't taken her long to observe that I was rather generous. When I did not have the means to lend some of my poor messengers money I would borrow the necessary from anyone in the office. Camilla wondered if I wasn't possibly too openhanded with these poor youngsters. I told her no, that one could never be generous enough with those in need. She was of a different opinion absolutely, which surprised me, since she had Negro blood in her veins and had come up the hard way. I tried to tell her that white people sometimes had it harder than

Negroes. This she strongly doubted. I told her I had been a panhandler, a beggar, a bum. She said I was *different*, that I had stooped to such levels because I wanted to be a writer.

She was extremely kind-hearted, and often helped me in odd ways. Sometimes I would say, "That was mighty white of you!" to which she would always retort, "You mean mighty *black!*" She added that she thought it something of a weakness in her people to be so willing to lend a hand. I replied by observing that I had not noticed that black people were so helpful with one another. I said I could not see that the blacks helped the blacks any more than the Jews helped the Jews or, for that matter, the whites the whites.

She seemed taken aback by my remarks. To make it worse I ventured to say that if I were pushed far enough I would not only steal but murder. This was too much for her Christian conscience. (She was a Catholic moreover.)

I mention these talks about black and white because thus far no one had openly said anything about Camilla's antecedents. One day, however, one of those rats who are to be found in every organization—ass-suckers is the name for them—discovered that my assistant was part Negro. And he promply conveyed the information to my boss, who was the general manager. This was the man who had hired me and who always treated me with deference.

Over the telephone he told me what he had learned about Camilla, adding in a hypocritical way, that "We all know the company has made it a rule never to employ black people. I think," he added, "we will have to let her go." He didn't say when or how.

I promptly told Camilla what had happened. Almost immediately she said, "Don't worry, Mr. Miller. I will go to see

Newcomb Carlton," the then president of the company and the one I suspected who had hired her in the first place. "He wouldn't *dare* to fire me," she added.

Sure enough, the next thing I knew Camilla was offered a job in a Western Union branch in Havana—a better job with more money.

If my memory serves me right she refused the job and resigned. What became of her I never knew for only a few weeks later I quit my job myself.

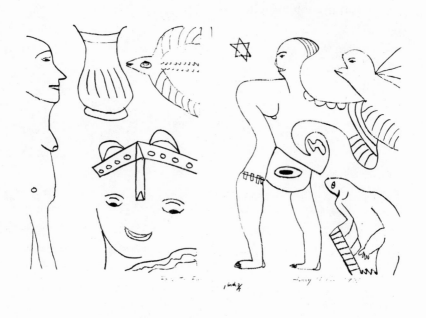

MELPO

Shortly after I returned from Greece I became a guest at the home of Gilbert and Margaret Neiman in Beverly Glen. The house they occupied was just a little shack off the road. It was there I began making watercolors for anything you wanted to give me—a dollar or two, an old coat, a pair of shoes, anything whatever. I was in terrible straits due to the banning of the books I had written in France. The idea of taking a job never occurred to me. I just kept on writing and painting little watercolors at night.

I was there only a couple of months when one day I received an unexpected visit from a Frenchman. He came to invite me to a reception being given by a Greek woman in some fashionable hotel a few miles away. He said she would send a chauffeur and limousine to fetch me. She was very eager to have me come as she had read my book on Greece and was deeply touched by it. He added that she was beautiful and generous. It wasn't difficult to convince me to accept the lady's invitation. The question was—what to wear? I had only the one suit for all occasions and it was worn threadbare. My shoes needed repairing. As I knew no one from whom I could borrow a suitable outfit I decided to go in what I had.

The hotel turned out to be rather a swanky one; the table

was set outdoors, there was a dance floor and musicians and most of the guests had already arrived.

The moment I arrived Melpo came forward to greet me. She was all smiles and expressed her gratitude for what I had done for her country. (She meant writing *The Colossus of Maroussi*.) I was so flattered my head began to spin. This before having any champagne. To my astonishment she insisted that I sit beside her at the dinner table as the guest of honor.

She was not only beautiful as the Frenchman had said, but full of grace and delicacy. In many ways she reminded me of Anaïs Nin from whom I was now definitely estranged. Like Anaïs she appeared frail but was actually quite strong and healthy. She was also extremely amiable. I had thought I would be too shy and awkward but she put me at ease immediately. It seemed to me she was trying to apologize for her wealth and the seeming ostentation. I sensed that at bottom she was simple, direct and uneasy with her riches. The Frenchman had told me she was the wife of a prominent Greek ship-owner, a rival of Onassis. That had frightened me a bit when he mentioned it but now here I was in her presence, and feeling perfectly at home.

It didn't take me long to discover that she was most intelligent and extremely well-read. She spoke four or five languages to boot.

How she learned it I don't know but she was cognizant of the fact that I was down on my uppers. This fact only drew her to me more closely.

When the music started up she turned to me and asked if I would like to dance. She had already pushed her chair back. Out of politeness I said yes but quickly explained that I was not much of a dancer. She said it didn't matter. To my surprise I found myself doing very well on the floor. Fortunately the dance music was old-fashioned. And I found I hadn't forgotten how to waltz or do the two-step. As we danced we talked; she volunteered or confided some surprising information about herself—to put me more at ease, I surmised.

Everything went beautifully. Before the evening ended she asked if she could accompany me home. She said she was a poor sleeper and used to being up all hours of the night. And so she escorted me to my dump in Beverly Glen.

On saying good-bye she asked if I minded if she were to drop by occasionally of an evening. She would like to take me for a spin and *talk* with me.

She would always telephone first to make sure I was free. Then her chauffeur and limousine would arrive to pick me up. Sometimes she would ask if she could have dinner with me. That always meant dining in some good modest restaurant. Before the meal was ended she would slip me the money to pay the bill under the table. It was usually double the sum needed. I said we loved to talk. She was an excellent conversationalist and always had plenty to relate. She had traveled over most of the globe—was equally at home in Rio as in London, Paris, New York or Tokyo. Our talk was always of books and places, two endless subjects. During all this time, and even later, I never so much as kissed her or embraced her. I venerated her. In the beginning she was surprised to learn I didn't have a car. "How do you get around?" she asked. "I walk," I replied. What walks! Back and forth to the Village, with a laundry bag slung over my shoulders. Up into the Hollywood Hills and back at 3 or 4 in the morning. Only once did a driver offer me a lift and that was a rather distinguished film director who was living with Marlene Dietrich at the time. The others who passed me by never gave me so much as a tumble. I was just another bum to them, I guess.

Well aware of my poverty stricken condition, Melpo nevertheless pretended not to be aware of it. Until one day I received a telephone call from her. It was almost a monologue. The burden of it was that she could no longer bear to see me living in such poverty, I who was one of the greatest writers in the world. I who had done so much for her people, and she who was so wealthy and had need of nothing. What she wished to do for me and, she insisted, it was the *least* she could do, was to get me a car, some new clothes, and put a modest sum of money in the bank for me.

Needless to say, I was so overwhelmed by her suggestion (or request) that I was almost speechless. I begged her not to do anything immediately, but to let me sleep on it.

And that night I had the strangest dream in all my life. I dreamt that God had deigned to talk to me. He was telling me not to worry, that He had an eye on me and that I would never again be in dire need. In fact, he added, you shall always have everything you need.

I don't mean to say that those were His exact words, but they were the gist of them. In a sense He told me much more, things I would blush to put on paper.

Naturally I awoke next morning not only stunned but jubilant. I called Melpo right after breakfast and related the dream to her, adding—"You realize now, I hope, that I can't accept your most generous offer. I don't really need a thing anyway. I have what most people lack and you know that. But I thank you from the bottom of my heart."

Shortly after this happening Melpo had to leave for New York to join her husband. A month or two later I had a letter from her from Paris. Once in a blue moon I hear from her. I believe she divorced her husband and was living with another man somewhere in the vicinity of Paris. We remain eternal friends. I hope she is still alive to read what I have written about her.

How wonderful, I think to myself, that I never attempted to make love to her. Could she possibly have offered me more by offering her body as well?

If it truly was God whom I spoke to in my sleep, then it most certainly was she who inspired God, sacrilegious though this may sound.

19.
/23

SEVASTY

I believe it was some time after knowing Melpo that I fell into the clutches of Sevasty. A friend of mine pointed her out to me at the library where she was working. He added, as if to clinch it—"She's Greek."

Yes, Sevasty was Greek but born in America. Her mother, who was about the same age as myself, happened to be also born on December 26, my birthday. Her mother was thoroughly Greek and somewhat fearsome—to me, at least.

The first mistake I made was to pronounce Sevasty's name wrong. I called her (on the phone) S*evas*ty instead of *Se*vasty.

I was still living in the little cottage (the Green House) in Beverly Glen. I was still poor as a church mouse, and it goes without saying, minus a car. Still footing it—no matter where.

Now Sevasty at that time lived somewhere in the Hollywood Hills—a distance of at least seven or eight miles. I was courting her assiduously and always on foot, as I have just remarked. It was an endurance test. Often I did not get home until 4:00 in the morning. Weary, footsore, and often defeated.

Yet we had great love scenes, either in the yard of her house or in the rear of the Green House. Passionate love scenes, which left both of us exhausted. Yet never any sexual intercourse, for Sevasty had an obsession about *not* making love. Seems she had only recently divorced a young Greek who was more like a stud horse than a human being. In addition she had undergone a hysterectomy and was mortally afraid of growing a beard and having piano legs.

I have not mentioned her looks or her figure—both ravishing and tantalizing. Essentially she was the embodiment of sex. Sometimes, in mushing it up with her, she would appear to swoon.

At this particular period there was also another guest (or freeloader) at the Green House and his name was Dudley. Tall, handsome, talented (he both wrote and painted). To Dudley my affair with Sevasty was something of a bad joke. He knew that she completely dominated me. And I made no bones about it. I was at her beck and call, as they say. One day when she had written or telephoned me to get in touch with her—I believe it was for 2:00 P.M. sharp—Dudley suggested that we go to a bar before calling her. At the bar he asked if I wanted to put up with her nonsense perpetually. And I of course answered "No!" "Then listen to me," he began. "See that big clock back of the bar? Let's wait till the hands say ten after two and then go home. Don't call her! Are you game?"

Though it was torture for me, I did as he had urged, and to my surprise, went back home with him feeling quite normal—in fact, I should say, *relieved*.

Next day I received a special delivery letter from her, just as Dudley had predicted, asking in sorrowful words if something had happened to prevent me telephoning her. She signed off "with much love." All of this was certainly a great *soulagement*, as the French say, but still I was under her spell. I ate, drank and slept Sevasty. It was Sevasty this and Sevasty that.

Everyone in the neighborhood was aware of my infatuation.

Then one day, like out of the blue, appeared a perfect stranger who said he would like to help me, if I would permit him. I said "How?" And he replied: "I would suggest that you have a talk with Swami Prahbavananda." I recognized the name, having been invited several times by ardent disciples to visit the ashram where the Swami lived and lectured.

"Why don't you telephone and ask if the Swami will see you?" said the stranger.

Why not? said I to myself. And so a few minutes later I picked up the phone and asked for the Swami. To my great surprise he answered the phone himself. "What can I do for you?" he asked immediately. I told him that I was in a desperate plight and needed very much to have a few words with someone like himself. To my utter amazement he responded by saying, "Come over at once if you can. I will be very happy to see and talk with you."

I made some excuse for not visiting him that afternoon and asked if he could possibly see me about ten o'clock the next morning. His reply was swift and cordial. "By all means," he said. "Come any time that suits you."

I went to bed that night somewhat elated. After all, the proposed meeting was exactly what I needed. I wanted someone to listen to me *seriously*.

Promptly at ten the next morning I knocked at his door. He opened it with a warm smile and started to shake hands with me. But I quickly informed him that I had only come out of politeness. I added that something had occurred during the night and my problem had disappeared. "I'm sorry," I said, "But I don't have any need of you now."

To which he quickly replied, "But how do you know *I* don't

have need of *you*." And so saying he grasped my arm and led me into his quarters.

I found that I had no need to go into details about Sevasty. I simply told him the problem had resolved itself in my sleep of its own accord. What I forgot to tell him was that his words, his manner of speaking over the phone had probably been the trigger which produced my release.

And so, as I said, we wasted no time on Sevasty and my foolishness, but began to talk of things of greater import. I remember telling him of my great love for Swami Vivekananda and Ramakrishna among other great souls. We rambled on for about an hour, pretty much as if we had known one another all our lives.

I left his presence feeling I had made a real friend. I remember particularly that he had scrupulously avoided urging me to attend the meetings, that he had shoved no propaganda on me. Instead he had accepted me just as I was, another human being.

A short time after this exhilarating event I found myself living in Big Sur, where I remained seventeen years.

I had married again and was the father of two wonderful children. After being in Big Sur about a year I received a letter from Sevasty asking if she could visit me. I naturally assented.

She arrived looking just as beautiful as ever but without the powers of seduction she had wielded before. I took her for a long walk through the woods, during which we engaged in a serious but most friendly talk. When she got ready to leave she turned to me with an expression I had never before observed and said, "You are not only a great writer but a great man."

The hero of the romance was of course the good Swami Prahbavananda. Bless his name!

AUNT ANNA

I must have been between twelve and fourteen when Aunt Anna, as my mother called her, first appeared on the horizon.

Actually she was not my aunt, nor my mother's. Perhaps she may have been something like a second cousin to my mother. In some mysterious way she was related to the woman my mother always referred to as a monster. And her brother was that halfwit whose arm had been bitten off by a horse—so the story went.

She was married to a local politician, a crude specimen, whom my mother detested. As a matter of fact, he was quite a decent sort, as I discovered later in life. Typical of the politician then and now. How he ever got to marry this angelic creature called Aunt Anna is beyond me.

There was something very special about Aunt Anna. (My mother, by the way, always referred to her as Annie, not Anna. Anna belonged to the aristocracy of Tolstoi's famous novel.) Anna's visits to our house were few and far between. My mother always seemed to spy her coming through the gate in the street. In an almost reverential tone, she would turn quickly to me and say: "O, Henry, Aunt Anna is here. Go to the door and open it for her!"

I of course would spring to my feet, only too happy to open the door for Aunt Anna. She would always embrace me warmly, which would make me blush. As I said, I was about thirteen and she was a woman in her late twenties. To me she had no age, nor sex either. She was simply angelic, not of this world. I suppose she was what is called beautiful, but I was impressed by other qualities which were not exclusively feminine. In short, she was of the airs, as the Greeks would say, a creature not only ethereal but possibly celestial.

All through her visit with my mother I would sit and stare at her. She was probably aware of my adoration for after she had finished talking with my mother she would address herself to me. And in a way that seemed (to me at least) very private. What we discussed I no longer remember but it seemed to be intimate, very confidential.

Before my eyes there sat a woman who was *different*. The difference was on the side of the angels. (This reminds me of seeing Greta Garbo many years after her stage and screen career had ended. It was one of her early films and I had brought with me an Israeli actress who had never seen a Garbo film. The moment Garbo appeared my young Israeli friend gave a gasp, as if she had been stabbed. As for myself, the tears quickly came to my eyes. I wept silently and unashamedly. I wept because of her most unusual beauty and also for her grace and skill as a performer.)

At the age I was at the time, I was still too young to be stage struck by any celebrities. I had never entered a good Broadway theatre, only the cheesy local ones which left no impression on me.

Why was Anna so different from other women I knew? Unfortunately the only women I was cognizant of were my mother's friends or relatives. Thinking of them (later) I remarked the differences in speech, in gait, in gestures, in posture. My mother's cronies were mostly Germanic, and in Brooklyn at that time the German element was not noted for grace and charm. Quite the contrary.

Yet Anna was of German descent and came from a most provincial suburb. But Anna spoke like an angel; Anna *looked* like an angel, if I may say so. Thoroughly feminine, there was that additional quality which set her off from others. Only a few years later and I would be stumbling on the works of that little known 19th century author, Marie Corelli. Anna belonged to the hierarchy of those extraordinary female characters whom Corelli invented out of the whole cloth. Most of them were tinged with divinity.

Whence came these creatures whom we are destined to meet usually only once in a lifetime? Like those unknown and most invisible creatures who swarm all about us and whom we sense not, so there are these earthly-heavenly bodies who influence our whole lives yet we fail to acknowledge them. In certain European countries there are what is known as "the little people." No one but the mad or the insane have ever seen or spoken to one, yet there is a tacit agreement among the common people that these mythical creatures truly exist.

All my life I wittingly or unwittingly have used Anna as a yardstick to detect others of her ilk. I have even had the great good fortune to live with one or two. Just as we can spot a holy man by the lustrous spherical orbs in his head so we can detect the presence of the angelic ones, no matter how they dress or look or behave.

Are we not more powerfully affected by the things or beings we refuse to acknowledge as real? Is it not precisely the unknown which leads us ever onward and upward? Goethe called it *"das ewige weibliche"* (the eternal feminine). We have the eyes to recognize them but not the sight. They are here among us "on loan," so to speak.

FLORRIE MARTIN

The Martins lived only a few doors away from us when we lived in "the old neighborhood"—Williamsburg, Brooklyn. Their daughter Florence and Carrie Sauer brought me to the police station one day for using bad language. Only my mother and her mother called her Florence. Everyone else referred to her as Florrie, which suited her better.

When we moved from the old neighborhood to "the street of early sorrows" in the Bushwick Section, we were soon followed by the Martin family, which included Ole Man Martin and his son Harry who was a year or two older than I, but slightly retarded for his age. Ole Man Martin, as everyone called him, was a character. He made a living working for the big hotels in Manhattan, which is to say, keeping them free of rats and mice. To do this he used two ferrets, which he carried in the pockets of his tan overcoat, a coat that only came to the knees and was already long out of style. His wife was an ardent church-goer with a sad and pious expression most of the time. Like my parents, she was a Lutheran. But my parents never set foot inside a church whether Lutheran, Methodist, Catholic or Presbyterian.

I was now about 16 or 17 and Florrie Martin must have been

97

23 or 24. She was attractive and very blonde. She would ask me to take her to the movies or to a dance or some festival or other. And always, in the vestibule of her home, she would give me a long, slobbery kiss. I was not used to that treatment from older women. It set me afire and made me a frequent visitor at the home of the Martins.

It must have been my last year in high school for I was already a member of the celebrated Xerxes Society. I was also a pal of her brother Harry who was something of a trial to his parents—a "loafer" and a "good-for-nothing," they called him. Harry took a liking to me and showed me "the other side of life," so to speak. It was through him that I first saw a burlesque show, the type which no longer exists. I was thoroughly shocked and completely enchanted; in fact I became an habitué of burlesque from then on. (And have never regretted it.) Harry also taught me to shoot pool and throw dice for drinks at the bar. It amused him to see me catch on so quickly.

The family were very friendly to any and everyone, at least so long as he or she was a church member. They always invited me to have coffee and cake or ice cream.

The more I saw of Florrie the more I adored her. She was always radiant, always helpful and never indulged in criticism as did my folks. Without realizing it I fell madly in love with her.

The Xerxes Society. . . . It was customary for us to meet at one another's homes once every two weeks or so. This time it happened to be at my house. Somehow this evening things didn't go off as usual. There was an air of restraint among the twelve members, provoked probably by my admonition not to make too much noise. I urged this much against the grain, only because my mother had begged me to have more consideration for the neighbors.

During a lull one of the fellows asked me if I wouldn't play for them. He said he heard that I was making fabulous progress at the piano. I readily agreed and sat down to play Liszt's "Second Hungarian Rhapsody," the only one of his I knew. I did it with verve and dash and to my amazement was roundly applauded. "Encore, encore!" they shouted. Flattered that they thought so well of my style, I consented to play another. This time it was either Schumann or Rachmaninoff. I forget which. I rather suspect it was Schumann because I remember that as I ended the piece I was in a very sober poetic mood—*hors de moi-même*, so to speak. Yes, I sat there a moment or two after the closing notes in a semi-trance. The music had enchanted me. This time the applause was less vehement. Suddenly the enchantment was broken by some raucous voice demanding to know if I still saw Florrie Martin and how was it going. This was followed by other voices, one asking me if I was getting my end in, another if she was a good lay. Soon all the club members began laughing hilariously. And with this I suddenly wheeled around on my piano stool and began weeping. Not just crying, but weeping and sobbing at the same time. One of the members came over to me, put his hand on my shoulder, and said—"Jesus, Hen, don't take it so hard; we were only joking!"

This brought on a fresh burst of tears and sobs. (Only two or three times in my whole life have I wept as I did that night.)

What had happened? What caused this display of emotion? Partly the music, I suppose, and partly the fact that my love for Florrie Martin was of a purity these callow idiots would never comprehend. But primarily, I would say, because I was an adolescent. And in many ways I have remained an adolescent all my life. (I didn't know until the other day, for example, that I was still capable of a similar show of emotion.)

"The age of puberty," I believe they call it. A period of total contradictions: one day hot, the next day cold; a fervid friend today, tomorrow a heartless son-of-a-bitch. And so on. The way older folk regard this period in their progeny is painful. They refer to it as "growing up," "becoming a man." Nothing could be farther from the truth. It is the period when one loses one of man's most precious qualities—*innocence*. And what a loss this is only poets know. To become a man in this stinking civilization is tantamount to becoming a rat. It means retrogression, not evolution.

All the knowledge and experience on which man sets such value seems to me like utter nonsense. Growth does not mean arterio-sclerosis. Growth means what the French call *épanouissement*. Indeed, a French saying sums it up to a T. *Pourri avant d'etre muri*. Rotten before ripened.

How strange, when I look back on this incident, that the Puritan in me should later have given birth to books that shocked the world. And yet perhaps not so strange. There is a Greek word which a learned friend of mine left with me as a little token of affection. It is *ENANTIODROMOS*. It means the process whereby a thing turns into its opposite, as for example, love into hate, and so on. May it not also be possible that we are never one but always two? How otherwise can we explain a Gilles de Rais, the valiant supporter of Joan of Arc, and the monster who emptied whole villages of young men or boys whom he raped and then murdered?

EDNA BOOTH

Edna was the first female writer in my life. We met in the Catskills (the Borscht route today) in a town called Athens where my parents had decided to spend the summer vacation.

Edna had a sister called Alice and I had a friend named George from my neighborhood in Brooklyn. We were about 16 or 17, the two sisters in their late twenties. We all resided at a boarding house, which was the custom in those days. It was the period of Rag Time and one of my favorite pieces which I rendered fairly well was "The Maple Leaf Rag."

The difference in age between us boys and the two attractive women didn't seem to matter except that no sexual intercourse was permitted by the women. (We were much too young, in their opinion.) But this did not prevent them from tongue kissing. Every night we met at the same secret place and held our "orgies" there. Orgy it was for me. I had never had anything to do with a woman as much older than I as Edna Booth. She was an expert at manipulating her tongue. (I couldn't even touch her boobs or her cunt—just this tongue kissing *ad nauseam*) and a warm embrace. Sometimes we broke the routine and took the girls (or women) for long walks during which Edna told us something about her writing and a great deal more about the books she had read.

And it is because of the books that I can never forget Edna Booth. Whether she had read the classics I don't recall, but she knew the contemporary best writers along with some of the 19th century ones like Balzac, de Maupassant, Ibsen, Strindberg, Gautier, Verlaine (not Rimbaud!) and so on. Her favorite American writer was Theodore Dreiser. She also knew a few of the great Russian writers, like Maxim Gorky and Gogol and Tolstoi, but not Dostoievsky. Nor did *I* at the time. This greatest of all writers (in my humble opinion) I only came to know a year or two later.

It was about five in the afternoon and the "event" took place at the corner of Broadway and Kosciuski Street, Brooklyn. I have told the story before, but I am not ashamed to repeat it. Mahler repeated himself, so did Chopin and Beethoven—why should I worry about what the "critikers" say? Anyway, I was passing a dress shop and in the show window stood a young man about my age who was dressing a model. He caught my glance and beckoned me to step in. Which I did. He gave me his name—Benny Einstein—and asked if I would wait a few minutes as he was quitting work and lived nearby. Maybe I would accompany him to his home? I readily agreed and in the space of a few minutes he suddenly popped the question—"Have you read Dostoievsky?" (He must have divined that I was a literary bloke!)

"Dostoievsky?" I repeated. "Never heard of him." I added that I *had* read some Russians but not this bird.

"You never read *Crime and Punishment?*" he blurted out. As if such a thing could not be.

"No," I confessed. "What else did he write?"

And so Benny went on to name the leading ones: *The Brothers Karamazov, The Possessed* and *The Idiot*.

I didn't realize till some weeks later what a heavy dose he had given me. Dear reader, if I seem to be making a fuss over a trifle, believe me I am not. Just as I never tire of recounting my accidental meeting with Emma Goldman in San Diego, so I never tire of rehearsing this introduction to Dostoievsky.

Looking back on the episode it seems to me that that late afternoon in Brooklyn the sun must have stood still in the heavens for a few moments.

But to return to Edna Booth. She in turn was amazed at all the authors I had read. And I had read a good deal for a guy my age. Particularly *foreign* authors, in translation of course.

Her sister Alice was quite a different type. She had auburn hair and freckles. Edna looked more like an actress and despite her sexy attitude held herself with dignity. I shall never forget how one afternoon I encountered Alice as we both were making our way through a field of oats or barley. As I bent forward to give her a friendly kiss I noticed a look of terror pass over her features *and*—suddenly she bolted. I immediately gave chase. Now Alice didn't hold the slightest interest for me—in fact, I took her for a nit-wit—but running away as she did, as if I were threatening to rape her, got my dander up. I ran and ran until I caught up with her. Then I took her by the arms, looked her square in the eyes and said: "You idiot, what's wrong with you? Did you think I was going to rape you?"

She hung her head and answered meekly, "Yes."

This only enraged me the more. For one brief moment I dallied with the idea of throwing her down and giving her a good fuck.

It wasn't her virtue that preserved her but her stupidity. I gave her one long look of disgust and turned on my heel to walk quietly back to the boarding house.

A little later that afternoon I ran into Edna. I said nothing about the incident with Alice. Instead I invited her to play a game of croquet with me. Croquet was still in fashion then. It's a game that a woman or a youngster can often play as well as a man. Somehow the chase after Alice had set my sexual glands working. As we moved from one wicket to another, as Edna bent over to pick up a ball or place a good shot I would deftly and gently fondle her rump. To my surprise she made no resistance. Because she was so much older than I and so much wiser I never dreamed one could take such an approach with a young lady. It was an eye-opener for me. It struck me later that the motto for such behavior should be: "Do it first and apologize later."

But with Edna there was no need to apologize. She knew me inside out, better than I knew myself.

The vacation over, we all returned to Brooklyn. Edna and her sister lived in some more aristocratic part of town than did my folks. We exchanged a few "literary" letters, and that was all. And then one bitter cold New Year's Day while out New Year's calling with the other members of the club (The Xerxes Society), who should I run across—in a trolley car—but Edna, her sister and father and mother. I was a bit embarrassed to be caught out with such louts and bounders but Edna gave it no never mind. She noticed that most of us carried musical instruments and so she graciously asked that we get out our fiddles and what not and play something we liked.

"What, *here* in the trolley?" we asked, or shouted rather, for we were all a bit lit up. "Certainly," she replied. "You're not breaking any law by playing music in a public conveyance." That said, we got out our instruments, tuned up and—"What will we play?" shouted one of the guys.

With that Georgie Gifford struck up, "We are such fine musicians . . ."

It made a hit with the passengers in the trolley. "More, more!" they yelled. And like that for fifteen or twenty minutes we regaled the bunch.

We only stopped because we were nearing our destination. As we stood up to go Edna beckoned me to approach. As I leaned over her seat to shake hands and say good-bye she pulled me to her and gave me a rousing smack on the lips. Then, under her breath, she added: "I've never forgotten Athens!"

Needless to say that did it for me. I drank like a fish everywhere we called that New Year's Day and tumbled into bed drunk as a pope.

I must add that much much later, when I visited the real Athens, I thought of Edna and the Borscht route. And of Dostoievsky whom she had not yet read.

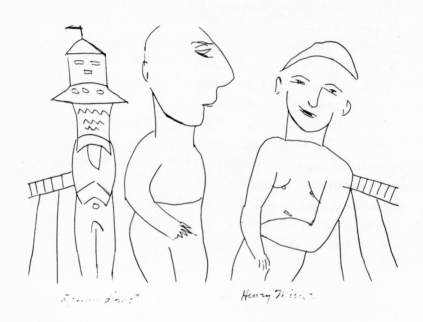

LOUELLA

I don't think Louella was her given name, I think she christened herself Louella because her real name was so difficult to pronounce. She came from a strange part of the world, one that few Europeans or Americans ever get to. As a matter of fact it was somewhere in the vicinity of Gurdjiev's birthplace. As a consequence she spoke a number of strange tongues—Armenian, Arabic, French, Turkish, Bulgarian, Russian and so on. And English as well. Indeed, her English was superb; she had been educated in a college somewhere in Lebanon, I believe. I never met her in the flesh but we corresponded regularly.

It began by my receiving a fan letter (with a photo) from her, after she had read *Cancer* and *Capricorn*. It was a fantastic letter, thoroughly perceptive, sensitive and beautifully written, in English, with lapses of French, Spanish and Portuguese. When I had these foreign language parts translated for me I discovered that she was not only well read, highly sophisticated, but somewhat of a sex addict as well. In fact, these passages sounded more like the work of a man.

I said we never met. She was constantly traveling, it seemed. And to the ends of the earth. One day I might receive a letter

107

from Hokkaido, the next from Tasmania or Rio de Janeiro. Nothing surprised me anymore.

She had an ebullient nature, always enthusiastic about life, but rather disheartened about the career she had chosen. It seems she had tried a number of fields, all of an artistic nature, and had finally wound up as a sculptress. Unfortunately, as she put it. She had very little talent for sculpture. She thought she might have done better to be a belly dancer or a night club singer. She was lucky not to depend for a living on her earnings as an artist. Just how she managed I never really knew, but I suspected it was through men. She had the morals of a bitch. *She* picked up the men she slept with and not vice versa. Except in one notable case. She claimed to have had an affair with Gurdjiev, maintaining that he had bewitched her.

A great part of our correspondence was centered about her attitude toward men—her sex life. She was perfectly frank about her tastes, her desires, etc.

For a brief period she wondered if she ought not try writing instead of her "half-assed sculptures," as she called them. She had read several books by Joseph Conrad and especially admired his use of English, which as is generally known, was the language he knew least well, yet he decided to write his books in this language. She asked what I thought of her English, to which I honestly replied that it was excellent. But then I added that that was no reason to choose it for her work. In fact, I urged her to write in some little known language, one she was proficient in.

"And who would translate me?" she demanded.

I answered, "Some scholarly Englishman, most likely."

She didn't like the idea of being translated. Anyway, after a series of letters discussing the possibility of her becoming a writer, she suddenly dropped the thought completely.

In many ways she might well have been dubbed "the Queen of Baluchistan." She was beautiful, exotic, gifted and a perfect snare for men. She lived not so much by her wits as by her cunt. She believed, or professed to believe, that God has given women cunts for two reasons—one for enjoyment and the other for survival. If she found herself short of cash and needed to take a cab she would seduce the cab driver. If a cop tried to give her a ticket for a traffic misdemeanor she would say "Tear it up! Let's go somewhere where we can have a private fuck!" And so on and so forth. Though she fucked for money—for a half dollar even—there was nothing of the whore about her. She thought the world was composed largely of idiots, bigots, and sadists. It didn't matter to her how she went about the business of survival. Only, no 9:00 to 5:00 job, please! *That* she considered insane. And so, as they say in burlesque—first she danced on one leg, then the other; and between the two she made a living. She took excellent care of her pussy. She knew all about the danger of venereal diseases but also knew that today they were curable without too much fuss. She was thoroughly realistic and at the same time an idealist. For example, in any sex relation involving love or affection she always did the choosing. The man had not only to be handsome, but virile and intelligent—a cultured gentleman, so to speak. And since she traveled here, there, and everywhere it was not too difficult to meet a man with her requirements. Sometimes they would remain together for months, especially if he were well-heeled and had charm. The one thing she could not abide was vulgarity. She had been over a good part of the U.S. and thought Texas the worst state of all. "Dumb brutes," she called the natives. Or "arrogant ignoramuses."

One may wonder, since we conducted such a long, drawn-out correspondence, why she never visited me. All during this time I was married and the father of two delightful children. Louella did not want to throw a monkey wrench into my domestic life. (She knew I would fall for her immediately.) Little did she know that it was the unhappiest marriage I had yet been through. Instead of the bliss she pictured, my life was more of an Inferno a la Strindberg. The only thing that kept me from suicide were my two children whom I adored.

So Louella kept knocking about the world, meeting men, having adventures of all kinds—in short, living life.

After not hearing from her for some time there came one day a letter from Guadeloupe. In it she related how she had met a handsome young woman about her own age, of mixed blood like herself, named Georgiana. Part of her blood strain was Irish, another part Creole. Apparently they were divinely suited to one another and soon established a lesbian relationship. "After all," she wrote, "I've had a bellyful of men with their stiff pricks. It's a beautiful change to have a woman friend with whom one is so compatible." She went on to add that Georgiana had induced her to try writing as a career. Her first project was a book about the Polish writer Joseph Conrad. Unfortunately she knew no Polish, but what Russian she knew was of help.

"Why Joseph Conrad?" I asked.

"Because," she replied, "he had chosen the language he knew least well to write in." As we all know, it was English. Also there was not much sex in his tales of the sea. She liked that too. She was getting fed up with sex. After all, she possessed a mind as well as a cunt. Why not use it?

The language she had chosen to write in was Portuguese. She thought it a rich language; besides, she admired the Portuguese people. They ran themselves down instead of puffing themselves up.

Good! I congratulated her on her choice of subject and of language and waited to hear more.

An interesting thing about the choice of language was that she almost chose Arabic. It was good for sex and for cursing, she wrote. But then how few people in "our" world knew Arabic. It would have been time wasted.

Well, it took even longer for the next letter to arrive. She was no longer in Guadeloupe. No, she had run into a wealthy man whose business was book collecting. He was also something of a scholar: read in Greek and Latin as well as the romance languages.

He had fallen in love with Louella at first sight. He had been slightly suspicious of her relationship with Georgiana but Louella quickly dispelled that by urging her friend to make advances to him, thus throwing him off the track.

They had left Guadeloupe as he had urgent business in Geneva. And so, after a month or so, they all went to live in the Ticimo region of Switzerland—Locarno and then Lugano. Indeed, it was from her picturesque descriptions of this famous region that some years later I made it my business to visit the region, staying in a modest hotel in Locarno. As I have said elsewhere it was a veritable Paradise. In fact, eventually I had to quit the place—it was just too good. This sounds like an improbable reason, and certainly very few people have the opportunity to put my words to the test. But one should never forget that Paradise is always more boring than Purgatory or Hell. We were not made to inhabit a Paradise; we are more at home in the hell we have created.

From here on our correspondence diminished. I assumed that if she were not head over heels in love with him she at least respected him, her husband.

After a year or so the husband suddenly died of a stroke. He left her his entire fortune, which was considerable. On her own now, and comfortably situated for life, she decided to resume her literary career. She finished the book on Joseph Conrad; it was translated into English, French and German. And from Conrad she went on to write of other prominent authors such as Hermann Hesse, Wasserman and Maxim Gorky.

About ten years later I received a cablegram from her friend Georgiana, saying that Louella had drowned in a swimming pool.

RUTH AND THE
FUR-LINED COAT

I had a strong feeling for her, not just because she was highly intelligent, an excellent reader, always pleasant and agreeable, but because of her name — *Ruth*. Though I have long forgotten the story of Ruth in the Old Testament, the name still rings a bell.

And this Ruth, who happened to be Jewish, resembled the Biblical Ruth for some reason. She was married to a dear friend of mine, one of the few geniuses I have known in my life. I don't think they were very happy together; they were temperamentally unsuited to one another. I was too good a friend of my genius friend to take advantage of the situation; I was content merely to drop in on them occasionally and spend an hour or two chewing the fat.

They were both great talkers. He could talk all night about art (he was a painter himself) while she enjoyed discussing books and authors. She knew I was trying to write and did all she could to encourage me. Often our discussions lasted for hours, in which case I was always invited to stay for dinner. In those days I depended a good deal on these chance invitations to dinner. Always a good talker, on days when I was starving I waxed exceedingly charming and loquacious. I talked my way

113

into a meal as easily as taking a walk around the block. A matter of survival. And though I was a sponger, I was always welcome, always well received. This habit of mine was put to good use during my early days in Paris, as I have recounted elsewhere.

In New York, especially when virtually penniless, it meant a great deal of walking as well as talking to get some food in one's guts. I have often remarked the similarity in this respect to Rimbaud's vagabond days. The amazing thing, now that I look back upon this distant past, was my ability to walk immense distances on an empty stomach, for often none of my friends were home when I called on them. The one object which stands out in my memory, like a scene from a nightmare, is the Brooklyn Bridge. How many times I walked it to and fro on an empty stomach! I was as familiar with the scenery at each end of the bridge as an artist is with his theme, whether writer, painter or musician. The worst was *returning home* on an empty stomach. Because that meant a deal of walking in Manhattan, going from one friend's house to another. Oftimes I began my return journey from somewhere in the 70th or 80th streets. Needless to say, in New York there was little hope of ever hitching a ride. As a matter of fact I never tried to beg a ride. Like the idiot that I was, I just put my head down thoroughly disheartened, thoroughly depressed.

All this by way of relating how one day toward evening, and knowing no way of getting a free meal, I took the last nickel I had and got in the subway headed for Ruth's place somewhere in the Bronx. (I was then living near Columbia Heights, Brooklyn.) Even by subway it was a long trip and during the ride I prayed to God that Ruth or her husband or his sister would be home when I arrived. (I never phoned people in advance of my coming for fear they would make some excuse to dodge me.)

Fortunately, they were all home and in good spirits. They were delighted to see me and immediately invited me to stay for dinner. That night Ruth cooked an exceptionally good meal, topped off by some excellent French wines.

Since Ruth and her husband were on good terms this evening, it was not difficult to launch into monologues and dialogues. We must have talked of everything under the sun. Ruth's husband was especially fond of the Russian writers— *and musicians!*—and spent considerable time praising their works. For her part, Ruth broke ground by talking of 19th century Yiddish writers whom she had read as a young girl. We were drunk not on the wine alone but on talk. (I think of this evening with fondness because such occasions are now a rarity.)

Needless to say, none of us ever looked at the clock. Suddenly I realized that I was a long way from home and made ready to go. It was mid-winter and I was wearing a fur-lined overcoat which one of my Hindu messengers had given me as a gift on returning to India. It was a bit heavy when walking any distance, but warm and snug.

I was still thinking of our discussions as I left the house and turned automatically in the direction of the subway. It was only when I got to the subway station that I realized that I had spent my last cent getting to the Bronx. I stood on the subway steps reflecting what to do. I should have returned to my friends and borrowed a nickel or a quarter but I felt ashamed to ask for anything after having been so royally regaled.

As I looked around me I noticed a cab rack at the curb. And with that I suddenly had an idea. I went up to the nearest cab, told the driver my story, and offered him the fur coat if he would drive me to my place in Brooklyn.

"*Do you mean it?*" he shouted, and with that he hopped out of the cab. I was already slipping out of the fur coat to see if it would fit him. He tried it on and it fit perfectly. He beamed all over.

Once again he said—"Are you sure you want to do this? Do you really mean it?"

I replied in the affirmative without a second's hesitation. After all I had another ordinary overcoat and a sweater at home.

"Ok" he chirped, "hop in!" Then, "Where did you say you lived? You'll have to show me the way once we cross the bridge," he said.

We rode a space, then suddenly he turned halfway round and exclaimed: "You know, Mister, you're a bit of a nut."

"I know that," I replied calmly.

"Are you a writer or something like that?" was his next query.

"Exactly!" I said. "You hit it on the head."

Silence for a while. Then he tallied off with this: "First I thought you might be gaga. But you talked like a gentleman and I couldn't find anything queer about you. Now that I know you're a writer I understand. Writers are queer birds. Maybe you'll make a story out of it one day. . . ."

I answered: "Maybe."

RENATE
AND THE ASTROLOGER

I was met at the Hamburg airport by Rowohlt's secretary, a charming black-eyed, black-haired young widow with Italian blood in her veins. She was escorting me to my hotel because Rowohlt himself had been suddenly obliged to leave town.

The next evening I had dinner with her in a restaurant at the airport. Neither she nor Rowohlt lived in Hamburg. His very modern publishing house was located in Reinbek-bei-Hamburg, a village about ten miles distant.

It didn't take me long to fall in love with Renate. She was full of grace, beautiful to behold, and had a noble or aristocratic touch to her. Her forte, I soon discovered, was language. Not languages, although she spoke three, four or five fluently and often did translations. No, her interest was in language itself, how it got that way, so to speak. Etymology was her cocktail. Needless to say, I was all ears when she opened up on her passionate subject.

She, on the other hand, had read most of my work, both in English and in French. In short, though something of a scholar, she did not present the typical picture of a German female.

I had gone to Germany to arrange for translations of *Tropic of Cancer.* I was also getting a rather handsome advance—for the first time in my life.

Everything seemed propitious and promising. Renate and I often ate out, and I must confess, tasted some excellent cuisines. The wines too were good.

It so happened that she had two sons about the same ages as my son and daughter who were now living with their mother in Los Angeles. Their mother had just divorced the man she ran away with when we were all living in Big Sur.

One day Renate asked me to go to Hamburg with her to meet a good friend who was an analyst *and* an astrologer. She thought I would find him rather interesting.

She was right. He was not only interesting but fascinating. Hitler had forced him to become one of his own astrologers. But not for long. Soon it was discovered he was giving Hitler false hopes. Suddenly he became an enemy of the Reich and had to flee the country. This fact, and his interest in Madame Blavatsky's work helped form a budding friendship with the man. I forget his real name, so will call him Schmidt.

A couple of months later, so it seemed to me, Renate and I decided to share our lives, together with our children. Consequently, it was decided that I should make a trip around Europe—France, Italy, Spain, and Portugal more particularly—to see if I could find a good place to live.

My old friend Vincent happened to be in town and announced at once that he would be only too glad to act as my chauffeur, interpreter, and secretary. (He knew about five languages well, having been a pilot for a commercial airline for some years. He had seen a lot of the world to boot.)

We started off blithely, touring Germany for its scenery,

then gradually visited the other countries. We were proceeding at a leisurely pace; for once in my life I was not short of money. I had written my own children about the project and kept sending postcards as we made our way along.

In the Midi or south of France I was offered several chateaux at modest prices. But they were all in a state of disrepair and besides I would have had to maintain a chauffeur and a retinue of servants, all out of the question. Each time we stopped at a village, no matter where, there was always something fascinating about the place. (Even Austria, which was not really on our list for a home, proved highly attractive, particularly the countryside.)

Naturally at every stopover I immediately rushed to the Poste Restante (General Delivery) to see if there was mail from Renate. Usually there was. I of course wrote her abundant letters, describing our impressions and adventures.

When we entered Venice, Italy, for some unknown reason I was stricken by a deep depression. It was so serious and so seemingly unwarranted that I decided to write a letter explaining my plight to Herr Schmidt in Hamburg. Perhaps he could put a finger on the sore spot?

Needless to say, though we roamed the city from end to end I saw hardly anything of this fabulous city.

A few days elapsed and then one day at lunch in a modest restaurant I suddenly realized that the depression was leaving me. I happen to glance at the big clock on the wall and the hands read seven minutes after 12 noon. I go to my room and write Herr Schmidt another letter. "Don't worry. Depression gone as suddenly as it arrived." Etcetera, etc.

In two or three days I get a special delivery letter telling me that the depression had left me because he, Herr Schmidt, had been *praying for me!!*

Punkt!

We continued on to Portugal, where I almost decided to settle (because the southern part of it reminded me strongly of Big Sur). Letters from Renate were tapering off. Now, as we started homeward to Hamburg, without having found a home to live in, I grew more and more dubious about Renate and her great love for me. In fact, by the time we reached the German border, I was almost frantic. I was sure she had fallen in love with some other man. I also felt terribly guilty over my unsuccessful trip. When we finally got to Reinbek I found a Renate who had become as cold as an iceberg. No other man in evidence either. No explanation. Just that it was all over.

Alors, que faire? Put my tail between my legs and take the first plane back to California. Now I had good reason to be depressed. What would my children say—after all the glorious pictures I had drawn for them of a new home in dear old Europe?

Some ten to fifteen years passed during which time we exchanged a few friendly letters and then one day, out of the blue, came *the* letter. I read it over three times. It was simply unbelievable.

Here's what she related. First, that she had never ceased to love me; second, that the real reason for giving me the go-by was because the analyst-astrologer, Herr Schmidt, had warned her that a life with me would be disastrous.

The strangest thing about it all was that I agreed with him. I had been through five marriages. What guarantee was there that I could make a success of a sixth or seventh?

A little later it dawned on me why Herr Schmidt's reasoning was sound. Looking back on my "many marriages," I came to realize that I was always primarily in love with my work. I was hopelessly married to my work.

And so I consoled myself with the fact that an "artist" should never marry. Adding, by way of sauce, "Marriage is the death of love."

Creative World- 'Henry Miller- 1973

BRENDA VENUS

How shall I paint her? In silver, gold, ivory or
what? After all the other portraits I have drawn of women what
new can I add? Well, love is always new, even the hundreth time
around. I said Love, not sex. One can include the other, but the
other can exist alone, unnourished except by physical desire.
Love is a flame that is nourished on all sides from all directions.
Anything or anybody can inspire it. Sometimes life alone is
sufficient. There is holy love and unholy love. All are legitimate.
All are beseeching the same thing — a response. And even when
there is no response, love can exist, a tortuous affair, but still a
yearning, a beseeching. Perhaps the case of unrequited love is
just as thrilling and terrifying as mutual love. I have known all
kinds. I deem myself fortunate to know this latest love, Brenda
Venus. It is a love which seems to be astrologically right. We
meet at all intersections, all conjunctions, all eclipses. We love in
our sleep as well as in our waking moments. We are mad with
love, to put it bluntly. How explain this miraculous and fortuit-
ous conjunction? How explain sunrise and sunset, flood and
drought? Things just happen. They happen in an aura of mystery. Everything, every being is enveloped in mystery. We
move from one mystery to another. Our very language is pure

mystery, or pure magic, how you will. And the language of love is the most impenetrable of all. It does not ask to be understood, just to babble.

Brenda is from a small town in Mississippi, thank God. Not far from the delta. She spent a few years in a nunnery in Biloxi, not far distant. Biloxi happens to be one of my favorite American towns. The Southern states are my favorite states. I fight the Civil War over, in my mind, again and again. Each time I am fighting on the side of the "rebels." My chief is the one and only General Robert E. Lee. In my fantasies the South never lost the war. The South was simply crushed by the North. But the Southerners were better soldiers, nobler, more courageous, more daring and inventive.

All this apropos the South long before the intervention of Brenda. I speak of it to explain my seeming infatuation for the young lady from Hattiesburg. She has been out of the South for some years now, attempting to be a figure in the movies. She has her idols, her stars, her *vedettes* and she aims to be another one of them. All of which means we see each other infrequently. We live on dreams, letters, telephone calls, much like other lovelorn. Only we are not "lovelorn." Lovestruck perhaps, but not lovelorn. Hungry but not famished, Yearning but not whining.

We also know one another telepathically. We come to each other's rescue just in the nick of time. We know how to heal wounds, balm aches and pains, play Jesus, Mary and Joseph and Jehosaphat, what what! Sometimes we incarnate the Holy one and the Evil one. Sometimes we are just Adam and Eve. We are never out of tricks. No, there is always lurking somewhere the shades of Dixie Friganza. We wait at gas stations, bus stops, and subway exits, just like everyone else. But we wait in hope and peace. We know what we wait for. And it comes, sometimes by parcel post.

How did we meet? What matter, we met. And we have been meeting ever since. What's more, our *souls* meet. They meet at will or haphazardly, but surely, truly, sublimely. We sustain one another. I keep her from falling apart; she keeps me from bursting at the seams. We mollify and jollify one another. We appreciate one another. She could drag me along the rich river bottom. I would not murmur. All I'd keep saying (to myself) is — "I love you, I love you." I have said it a thousand times to a few hundred women perhaps. It is one phrase that never wears out, never gets rusty. To wake up with words of love on one's lips — what bliss! Just to say "Brenda" puts me in ecstasy.

Sometimes she talks Southern fashion to me. Then it's all moonlight and roses, camellias, gardenias and water moccasins.

To love at the end of one's life is something special. Few women can inspire that sort of love. Brenda seems to anticipate my wishes, my very thoughts. She is not bashful in avowing her love. She has guts, is quick on the trigger, ingenious. And always smiling. Not that fatuous smile of the empty head. A noble smile, sometimes a smile tinged with joyous sadness. Yes, she is a bundle of contradictions. Like myself. Maybe that alone explains a great deal, why we get on so well together, why we seem to have been made for one another since way back.

Did I mention that among other strains she has Navajo blood in her veins? That accounts for much of her character as well as physiognomy. Her silence is always impressive. Not gloomy, but meditative and speculative. It can also be chilling, as with our American Indians. Above all, she has a sense of fortitude, of independence, of determination. She can stand alone. She can use weapons with skill. She is not afraid of animals. She could kill without batting an eyelash, if she were obliged to kill. She can love the same way. Alors, what more does one want?

Inside she is like a three-ring circus. Always planning, intriguing, concocting. A perpetual ferment at work. Works herself to the bone physically and mentally. Can eat like a tigress but can do without too. Loves luxury but needs little. Is always dressed like a rainbow. Under the shower she sparkles. When snoozing, the dreams which float through her head keep her perpetually bedazzled. She is a volcano in restraint, a geyser holding back its stream or flame. Everything under control, yet wild as a tornado within.

Where will this strange creature lead me, I wonder? To what strange shores? I have put myself in her hands. Lead me, O blessed one, wherever!

Finis.